Ishq Sufiyana

Untold Stories of Divine Love

Ab Lafz o Bayan Sab Khatm Huye,
Ab Lafz o Bayan Ka Kaam Nahin!
Ab Ishq Hi Hai Paigham Apna,
Aur Ishq Ka Koi Naam Nahin!

GHULAM RASOOL DEHLVI

BLUEROSE PUBLISHERS
India | U.K.

Copyright © Ghulam Rasool Dehlvi 2025

All rights reserved by author. No part of this publication may be reproduced, stored in a retrieval system or transmitted in any form or by any means, electronic, mechanical, photocopying, recording or otherwise, without the prior permission of the author. Although every precaution has been taken to verify the accuracy of the information contained herein, the publisher assumes no responsibility for any errors or omissions. No liability is assumed for damages that may result from the use of information contained within.

BlueRose Publishers takes no responsibility for any damages, losses, or liabilities that may arise from the use or misuse of the information, products, or services provided in this publication.

For permissions requests or inquiries regarding this publication, please contact:

BLUEROSE PUBLISHERS
www.BlueRoseONE.com
info@bluerosepublishers.com
+91 8882 898 898
+4407342408967

ISBN: 978-93-7018-300-1

Cover Design: Sadhna Kumari
Typesetting: Pooja Sharma

First Edition: January 2025

Foreword

I am not a Muslim and I am not Indian. Therefore, having someone like me might seem like a rather strange choice to write a foreword for a collection of stories about Sufis in India.

But it should not be, for Muslim or not, Indian or foreigner, the tales within this book speak to everyone, regardless of faith or nationality. For, at their heart, they are, as Ghulam Rasool Dehlvi states in his introduction, tales of love. And love is something that all of humanity shares.

I first encountered love in a religious context in the Gospels. In the actions and stories of Jesus Christ as He taught His followers whilst walking around Galilee. At first, like many people, I thought such love was exclusive to my faith alone, but life and travel have taught me otherwise. **When I read stories like those in this book, I recognise the teachings of Christ, but also the Janamsakhis of Guru Nanak, the exploits of Krishna, and the lives of the Boddhisatvas.** And I am reminded of the shrines that I have visited and prayed at. The Sufi dargahs of India and Pakistan, the saint's tombs of Europe, the Buddhist monasteries of Japan, Varanasi, Haridwar and the Golden Temple in Amritsar. For the language of love crosses all borders and is eternal. As the Beatles once sang, "love is all you need."

And that message matters, especially in these days of division where demagogues try to deny our universal humanity and divide us into camps. Their path is that of fearing god, not knowing Him, of forcing others to be like them rather than befriending and learning from them. I pity them in their darkness.

Our God is wadud – the God of light and love. You can be Christian, Hindu, Muslim, Jewish, Sikh or Buddhist, but whatever path you approach Him by, He is ready to welcome you with open arms.

As one of the greatest Sufis of them all once said:

"Out beyond ideas of wrongdoing and right-doing, there is a field.

I'll meet you there."

- Rumi

- Matt Pointon

British Author and Explorer of World Mysticism, President of the Workers' Educational Association Global Interfaith Activist

Prologue

Bawa Muhaiyaddeen said:

"If each of you will open your heart, your actions, your wisdom, and your conduct and look within, you will see that every face is your face, every nerve is your nerve, each drop of blood is your blood,...all hunger is your hunger, all poverty is your poverty...all lives are your life. You will experience this in your nerves, in your body and in what you see. When that state develops inside you, that is the Divine Love...If that love develops you will not hurt any other living thing, you will not cause pain, you will not reject any life, and you will not torture any other life, because if you hurt anyone it will hurt you."

- Book of Gods' Love, p.23.

The values, virtues, and wisdom of the lives honored in **Ishq Sufiyana: Untold Stories of Divine Love** remain very much alive today. Remembering people of such attainment is inspiring. The power of transformative living love is a gift from God that continues to pour forth upon anyone whose heart opens to its mystery. It is important that we take their examples and bring their teachings into practice. That is where values become alive.

I write this for you as an American blessed to be learning from the Sufi Path of Love and its illuminating wisdom. The Sufi message is not bound by time, place, religion, or culture. It remains open today. This path was opened to me by the living example of the Sufi Saint

Bawa Muhaiyaddeen, who lived so humbly that he called himself an 'ant-man'. Others identified him as Qutb, Sheikh, or Guru. He lived affirming with every breath that only God is real, and God is One.

He was "discovered" in the jungles of Sri Lanka mid 20th century, taught there for decades treating all lives as beloved family without differences of religion, class, ethnicity, race or gender. He came to the United States in 1971 and through tireless service spread the core message that love is the path to God and that God lives in the human being and the human being lives in God. He established a Fellowship, a mosque in the Qadiriyya tradition, and there is also now a place of profound remembrance, a mazaar, near Philadelphia, Pennsylvania where people of all faiths are nourished. He demonstrated that Islam is founded on compassion for all lives as one's own and that such truth is not bound by any religion.

I share this testimony that transformative living love is not a mere expression of a poetic aesthetic from decades ago in another time and another place. It resonates within creation today and is available to each of us, now.

I bear witness that in this "modern" time a human being walked amongst us and affirmed that it is the birthright of every human being to realize peace, bliss, and the wisdom that liberates from ignorance, divisiveness, arrogance, and fear and affirms the reality of God. He demonstrated with clarity the path to such a state of fulfillment isselfless love. This emphasis is consistently found in the lives of Sufi Saints.The histories in this wonderful book remind us that people can attain the greatest of human achievements through selfless duty and perfected qualities. This is consistent with similar towering figures of purity and goodness found in all spiritual traditions, both today and in the distant past. As the Reverend Martin Luther King, Jr said in his Nobel Peace Lecture:

"Love is somehow the key that unlocks the door which leads to ultimate reality."

As Jesus emphasized, this quality of love cannot be separated from God. Our duty is to bring this treasure that makes us human into action in our relationships with all fellow beings.

Bawa Muhaiyaddeen often said: "Separate from yourself that which separates you from other lives." The same qualities that separate us from other lives – such as anger, fanaticism, falsehood, pride, jealousy, greed, hatred, hastiness -- separate us from the immeasurable power of goodness that creates, sustains, and absorbs all lives beyond name, gender, and form called Allah, or God. The same qualities that bring harmony with other lives – such as, love, compassion, tolerance, peacefulness, patience – bring us into harmony with our self and its source. That harmony ultimately awakens wisdom which can investigate the meaning of our lives. How glorious, unifying and full of justice is this mystery known only to those who open their hearts with compassion. If we do not learn such principles of harmony and put them into practice, we face a world ruled by the law of power, rather than the power of law; a world ruled by the love of power, rather than the power of love.

This love is without a form or limit. It is fulfillment. What is the evidence of such anattainment? Living a life of treating all lives as oneself, ethically, practically and experientially, and knowing that we live within God and God lives within all of us. I observed this quality in a human being as follows:

It was a very hot day in Jaffna, Sri Lanka in 1974. I was sitting at Bawa's bedside in his very humble ashram. He was very old, and the ashram was made up of a cement floor, a corrugated steel roof, and a courtyard ten yards from his bed with a variety of animals that included a goat, peacocks, a dog, a cat and a deer that had followed him out of the forest. The deer was always attentive when Bawa would sing and pray. Bawa's day consisted mostly of sitting on his bed and giving advice on understanding the wonder and beauty of God.

Because he was respected as a living saint, people attributed many things in their lives to him, both good and bad, which sometimes included events that should not have been attributed to him. One day a young man came in absolutely shaking with rage and hatred. Some tragedy had befallen his family and he was blaming Bawa. I was sitting right by the bed, and this fellow burst into the ashram screaming at Bawa while brandishing a machete, the kind used to cut bamboo.

I was close to him, close enough that I could have punched him. Surely he wouldn't have expected it. But my conscience said that it was not for me to step in front of the sage; in that moment I was to restrain myself—to be, not an actor, but only a student. This observing role was not my nature, but this inner message was very powerful. I was to watch but not engage. It was an odd very calm feeling.

Bawa attributed all beauty, goodness, wonder and the miraculous events that happened in creation only to God. He never centralized any events to himself. He did not use miracles as a way of promoting wisdom. He promoted the supremacy of love and the consciousness that comes from that love, as the pathway to human realization. In fact, he often stated that to know God one must go beyond the state of the "you" and the "I" and live with unity with all lives. Bawa lived what he taught.

So, as the enraged fellow raised his machete, as if to strike, Bawa opened his arms fully wide. He was very old, very thin, and as the weather was very hot he had on no shirt. He tilted his head sideways and back, exposing his neck fully to this flood of aggression and anger and with melting eyes of gentleness looked at the assailant and said:

"MY BROTHER, WILL TAKING MY LIFE GIVE YOUR SOUL THE PEACE IT IS SEEKING?"

Then, it was as if the molecules in the room began to scintillate and vibrate with the power of love. That love just filled the space we were in as a tangible presence. The man with the machete became like a puppet whose strings had been cut.

He collapsed on the ground, dropped the weapon, and gazed into the sage's eyes. Bawa then embraced him with complete kindness and compassionate understanding of his inner state. With motherly absorption, he said: "Go home and clean yourself, and come back, my child." At that moment, I had witnessed a human being respond to ultimate violence without concern for his own life—acting only for the well-being of the other. I saw the power of divine love in action within this world, and I learned the value of a true human being.

This event took place in this modern era. It is a timeless lesson arising from the ethics in action founded on the highest wisdom. This wisdom is realized in the ripeness of pure divine love.

Here is how I understand what he taught me, the realization which I am now striving to live. Love is, all at once, a Noun, A Verb, and Reality.

It has names but all its names only suggest its majesty.

The world today faces numerous problems that are caused by human conduct—institutional, organized, intentional conduct—which impacts every individual life. The powers of modern man over the natural world dwarfs that of all previous generations. The reach of human desires and aspirations far outstrip our moral vision and any sense of wise restraint. Too many millions of people live in fear. When the heart hardens, the blaming starts—the blaming of others for our own inner unrest. While many are living in abject poverty, the world's governments expend over $2 Trillion per year on multitudinous weapons, all in the pursuit of peace and security. Wars continue and the magnitude of threats expand. We can do much better. We must do better. We must be the example of what that means.

We have developed science which results in technologies that are melting the polar ice cap and impairing the regenerative processes of nature. In contrast, the lives of these Sufi Saints can show us a technology to melt the human heart. This is the most important technology the world needs today. This is what Sufi Saints taught then and that remains relevant today. More than relevant, it is necessary.

- **Jonathan Granoff**

President of the Global Security Institute, an international lawyer working to advance peace and security at all levels.

Preface

I first read the reflections in this collection by Ghulam Rasool Dehlvi Ji as they appeared in the daily 'The Asian Age'. I used to look forward to reading them and musing on their enlightening message. In fact, I started clipping and collecting them as well. They were more than food for thought. They were food for the spirit and a service to all readers. All faiths have this dual character that they have in them what can bind you and what can liberate you. That which binds is particular: that which liberates is universal. It appeals to the higher nature of all humans and not just to co-religionists.

This is the secret of enlightenment, harmony and mutual respect which should bind the entire human community. Dehlvi Saheb provided course after course of this elevated fare in a banquet without end, which now appears in the form of 'Ishq Sufiyana' for all to savour.

I suggested to Dehlvi Ji, why not put it all together in this grand feast. The readers can then treat themselves to any course at will and repeatedly so. That reading 'Ishq Sufiyana' can be so absorbing is not without reason. They reflect both deep learning and understanding of the realm of divine love, which only the truly gifted possess. All readers will be full of gratitude to Dehlvi Saheb for sharing this precious gift with us which both enriches our spiritual insight and lifts our spirit. Life is all about how much we can manage to refine our sight – 'drishti' or 'binai'. We should be grateful to Ghulam Rasool Dehlvi Ji for helping refine ours.

- **Kamalesh Sharma**

Secretary-General Commonwealth, Chancellor Emeritus, Queen's University Belfast

Contents

Introduction 1

Love has no Space for Fear 9

Rabi'a's Creed of "Unconditional Love" 15

Ishq-e-Rasool The Deep Divine Love 22

The Mystic of Mehrauli Martyr of Divine Love 25

The "Mahbub-e-Elahi" Beloved of the Divine 28

"Eid-e-Gulabi" A Sufi Celebration of Colours! 34

Sufi Basant: A Symbol of Multicultural Mysticism 38

Music & Mysticism— Makhdoom e Simnan &
Sufi Sima'a 43

Krishna in Sufi Mysticism The Prophet of Divine Love .. 50

The Divine Lovers Sees in Ram, Rasool! 56

An Abode of Spiritual Symbiosis— My Visit to
Ayodhya 61

In the City of the Most Beloved Madina Munawara 66

The Martyrs of Divine Love 70

An Untold Story of Divine Love 75

Baba Farid—Punjabi-Sufi Saint and his Pursuit of
Peace in Palestine 81

Hasrat Mohani and his Syncretic Divine Love 84

Sufi Music—Listen to language of Divine Love! 87

India, the the Land of Mastkalandars–the Divine Lovers 89

India in view of Amir Khusrau 91

Shah-e-Hamadan The saint who gifted Sufism
to Kashmir 96

Lalded/Lalla Arifa The Shaivite-Sufi Divine Lover 101

Mahbub-ul-A'alam—Beloved of the World...................... 105

Kashmir's Nund Rishi— A Mystic Master for All.......... 108

Ghaus Gwaliyari—The Shattari-Sufi Mystic................... 114

Dard's Divine Poetics 117

Aaina-e-Hind—The Divine Radiance in Bengal............. 120

Bu Ali Shah Qalandar— Fragrance of Ali Maula............. 123

Bulleh Shah— Pierced by An Arrow of Divine Love..... 128

Blessings for the Book... 131

Introduction

What is "Divine Love"?

Ishq-e-Elahi—The Sufi Notion of 'Divine Love'!

Ishq-e-Elahi (Divine Love) is the Sufi Interpretation of the Broader Qur'anic Notion of "Al-Hubb-u-Fillah" (Love in pleasure of Allah) or "Hubb-e-Ilahi". When Khwaja Gharib Nawaz Moinuddin Chishti—the most famous Sufi saint of India— left this worldly abode, his disciples saw the following Arabic words vividly written on his blessed forehead:

Hada Habib-u-llah Mata Fi Hubb-i-llah

This is the Beloved of Allah who died in love of Allah!

Baab-e-Jannat, Dargah Khwaja Moinuddin Chishti at Ajmer Sharif, Rajasthan

In the Indian subcontinent, the word *Ishq* in pop culture and Urdu and Punjabi literature has been much misconstrued.

The meaning of *Ishq* has been borrowed from medieval Arabic poetry, in which it was extensively used for something melancholic and romantic and sometimes a complete madness and craziness for a human being. For instance—going by the authentic Arabic lexicon, Lisan Al-Arab, "Ishq is an excessive Hubb, an abundance of it to the extent of excess". It says: Abu Al-Abbas Ahmed bin Yahya was asked about the distinction between Ishq and Hubb and was questioned: Which one is better? He said: Hubb because Ishq is replete with madness. Ibn Faris, the eminent Arabic philologist and lexicographer said: "Ishq" is an adoration of someone particularly a female, to the extent of being excessive in her love in complete blindness from realising her flaws.

However, in Sufism this is called "Ishq e Majazi", a state of love – 'pseudo-love' which is always meant to end in abandonment or desolation, as it is a material love and not an eternal affair. The mystical understanding of *Ishq* in Sufism is that it is a deeper state of love, and it is indeed the excess of it, the full indulgence in it, not for material love, but rather for real and esoteric love (Ishq-e-Haqiqi).

The Arabic word *"Hubb"* which entails the vast meanings of affinity, longing and love, has been used in the Qur'an for the same meaning that *Ishq* connotes in Sufism. In fact, the Arabic-origin term "Ishq" is the ultimate and highest culmination of Hubb which leads to self-annihilating surrender and complete submission to the Will of the Beloved Divine. Thus, viewed from this perspective, Islam in the sense of "submission to the will of Allah" is all about unconditional and infinite divine love for the sake of Allah in which there is no space for hatred or prejudice for anyone. This has been systematically expounded in the famous Hadith-e-Jibril which is also called "Ummul Ahadith" (The Mother of all Hadiths) in which Ihsan (spirituality or mysticism) has been rendered as the utmost perfection of Iman and Islam.

However, the Holy Qur'an only uses the Arabic term "Hubb" but not the word "Ishq", famously known in Urdu poetry and Persian literature to denote divine love. In many of its verses which talk about love for Allah, including the below-mentioned two pieces of long verses, the Qur'anic term of "Hubb-e-ilahi" has deep connotations Let us take a cursory look at them as follows:

(1)

قُلْ إِن كُنتُمْ تُحِبُّونَ اللَّهَ فَاتَّبِعُونِي يُحْبِبْكُمُ اللَّهُ وَيَغْفِرْ لَكُمْ ذُنُوبَكُمْ ۗ وَاللَّهُ غَفُورٌ رَّحِيمٌ

Translation: Say, [O Prophet], "If you should love Allah, then follow me, [so] Allah will love you and forgive you your sins. And Allah is Most Forgiving and Most Merciful. (3:31)

(2)

وَٱلَّذِينَ ءَامَنُوٓا۟ أَشَدُّ حُبًّا لِّلَّهِ

Translation: "And the (true) believers are those who love Allah more than anyone or anything else….." (02: 165)

In both the above crucial places, the Arabic term "Hubb" not "Ishq" has been used in the Qur'an. Hence, the greatest Sufi mystic and propounder of Wahdat ul Wajud (Unity of the Being) Sheikh e Akbar Mohiuddin Ibn ul Arabi and later his adherents among the Sufis frequently used "Hubb" following his footsteps. For instance—Ibn ul Arabi compiled an anthology of his poetry on the Divine Love (Ishq-e-Ilahi) and named it "The Translation/Translator of the Desires.

In this book, Ibn ul Arabi makes use of the Qur'anic term "Hubb" in an unconventional way, which goes against the mainstream hermeneutical theological tradition of Islam. He expands the meaning of "Hubb" to the Unconditional Love and thus incorporates the elements of "Ishq" in it. Look at the following Arabic couplet attributed to him:

أدين بدين الحب أنّى توجهت ركائبه، فالحب ديني وإيماني

Translation: {My heart has opened unto every form} I follow the Religion of Love. Wherever its caravan goes, love is my religion, love is my love and faith.

However, Persian-speaking Sufi poets and philosophers, especially Maula-e-Rum Jalaluddin Rumi and those who adopted Rumi's school of Sufi mysticism in the Indian subcontinent in Persian and Urdu poetry have frequently employed the romantic term "Ishq". However, their interpretations of Ishq are myriad. For instance—Sakhi Sultan Muhammad Najeebur Rahman called Sultan ul Ashiqin (the king of divine lovers) writes in his book "Shamsul Fuqara" in an explanation of the above Qur'anic verse:

"Hubb is the hallmark of a true believer, but Ishq is the beginning and the source of all creations. When the souls were created by the Light of the Prophet (Noor Mohammadi), Ishq-e-ilahi was ingrained in the human souls as an integral part."

He then refers to the prophetic tradition where he is reported to have said:

لا يؤمن أحدكم حتى أكون أحب إليه إلى آخره

One can't be a believer unless s/he loves the Prophet more than everyone. Sakhi Sultan further says: Hubb or Muhabbat can occur with anyone but Ishq is not possible except for Allah. When Hubb intensifies, it turns into Ishq, which is only for Allah. It is this Ishq-e-Haqiqi which makes you restless, and you willingly bear and enjoy all pain and sufferings unless you achieve the ultimate union or merger with the divine. Rumi elucidates it in a persian couplet:

عشق آں شعلہ است کہ چوں بر فروخت

ہر کہ جز معشوق باشد جملہ سوخت

Translation: 'Ishq' is a flame. When it flares up, it sets everything ablaze except the Beloved.

Here I am reminded of an Urdu couplet, unmindful of the poet who said it:

عشق معشوق، عشق عاشق ہے

یعنی خود آپ ہی میں گم ہے عشق

Ishq Mashuq, Ishq Ashiq Hai

Yani Khud Aap Hi Mein Gum Hai Ishq

It denotes that Allah is Himself Ishq (Love), Ashiq (Lover) and Ma'ashooq (The Beloved). Thus, He is actually immersed in Himself. Now contrast the above Urdu couplet with the following Arabic couplet which has a historical significance:

هذا حبيب الله مات في حب الله

Translation: He is a Habib-ul-Allah (The Beloved of Allah) who died in the love, Hubb of Allah.

The context of this couplet is that when the greatest Sufi saint of the Indian Subcontinent Hazrat Khwaja Moinuddin Chishti R.A passed away, the above Arabic words were divinely written on his forehead. This also points to the Sufi adage that "Al-Hubbu Fillah" (love for the sake of Allah) leads to "Fana Fillah (immersion and self-annihilation in the Divine) and consequently "Baqa Billah" (immortal existence with the Divine), which is the ultimate reality of Ishq-e-Elahi. In Sufism, it was beautifully embodied and epitomised by the Divine Lovers like Mansoor Hallaj in Iraq and Sarmad Shaheed in India. They truly exemplified the Union with the One in an abundance of Divine Love

The rules of Divine Love which form the bedrock of Sufi mysticism are as follows: Belief in *tawheed* (oneness of God), *ishq-e-Rasool* (unconditional love for the Prophet saw), *wahdatul wujud* (unity of existence), *ilm ul yaqeen* (knowledge with firm faith), *zikr* (incantation), *muraqaba* (meditation), observance of *taqwa* (God-consciousness) and *tawba* (repentance on sins), *ikhlas* (sincerity), *tawa-kkul* (contentment), *sidq* (truthfulness), *amanah* (trustworthiness), *istiqamah* (uprightness), *sabr* (patience), *shukr* (thankfulness) and *sulh-e-kul* (reconciliation with all).

Sufis were the harbingers of *sulh-e-kul*, a Persian term that essentially means: peace and reconciliation with all or "love for all and malice towards none" in the words of Khwaja Gharib Nawaz. This greatly impacted their attitude towards other faith traditions. They were loved by one and all; Kings and commoners, elites and laymen, intellectuals and illiterate and the poor and the rich were equally enchanted by the immense sincerity and simplicity in their lives. This appealed to one and all, regardless of caste and creed.

Love has no Space for Fear

Divine Love is 'fearless' and it shows God's love for mankind as infinite, all-inclusive and all encompassing!

Once, Prophet Muhammad and his companions saw a mother bird with her babies in a nest. She was feeding worms to her babies. Her actions were so loving, tender and gentle that the companions were pleasantly surprised at the display of her natural love. This beautiful and fascinating scene reminded the Prophet of infinite love and mercy of

God for all mankind and, therefore, he smiled and asked his companions:

"Are you surprised at the love this mother bird shows to her babies? Let me tell you that God loves man 70 times more than this mother!"

This Prophetic tradition shows God's love for us human beings as infinite, all-inclusive and all encompassing. Not a single creature is exempted from His bountiful grace and divine mercy. The Holy Prophet explicitly said, "When God created His creatures, He wrote in the book: 'Verily, My mercy prevails over My wrath.'

From time immemorial, there have been two diametrically different faiths in the world. One stresses that God is *wadud* (the all-loving and all-embracing). Al-Wadud, one of the 99 names of God in the Qu'ran, shows that He is truly forgiving, all-embracing in His love, as is enunciated in Surah Al-Buruj. Going by this, those who believe that "God is love" embrace a world of differing religions and are devoted to saving rather than destroying humanity.

Secrets of Divine Love draws upon the spiritual secrets and divine mysteries of the Qu'ran, mystical poetry and stories from the world's greatest prophets and spiritual masters to help us reignite our faith, overcome our doubts and deepen our connection with God. Practical exercises and guided meditations help us develop the tools and awareness to overcome the inner impediments that prevent us from experiencing divine love and attaining a close personal relationship with God.

Thus, God's all-encompassing love prevents us from falling prey to fear and grief. Rather it turns grief into bliss. The friends of God have no fear, whatsoever, nor do they grieve, says the Qur'an (10: 62). Another Qur'anic anecdote which immensely inspires Sufi mystics to overcome fear in divine love is this "La Yakhafuna Lawmata Laim" (Surah Al-Maida 5:54). This implies that Divine Lovers do not fear the reproach of the reproachful. They are not afraid of any blamer's blame in their path of fearless love And they are unafraid to speak the truth, come what may. Rather they go to the extent of inviting such criticisms, which ultimately draw them closer to the Divine 'friends' (Awliya Allah) and further away from His 'foes'. It can be explained by this pertinent couplet in Arabic which offers a similar notion of fearless and courageous love that Sufi mystics like Rabi'a have espoused. It says:

أحبه و أحب فيه ملامة | إن الملامة فيه من أعدائه

Translation: I love Him and I would love every taunt and insult in this love. For such insults only come from His antagonists and enemies.

Shrine of the 13th century Sufi saint Lal Shahbaz Qalandar in Sehwan Sharif, Pakistan

This notion of fearless love serves as a compass and guiding light that connects a divine lover to the source of eternal peace and complete submission and surrender to God's will. Psychologically, they are healthy human beings and pose no threat to any section of society. They also espouse and epitomise the beautiful spiritual principle of "love for all and hatred for none" deeply embedded in Sufism. Inspired by the Qur'anic teaching "to save a life is to save the whole mankind" (Surah Al-Ma'idah: 32), they exert every possible effort to protect human lives even if they have to lay down their own lives for others. They seek to prevent violence, bloodshed and unjust killings in various parts of the world to preserve human dignity.

On the contrary, the other group of believers propound that "fear of God" should be given preference over love for Him. This line of thinking paves the way for those who play the role of takfiris or crusaders forcibly imposing "God's will" apropos their own concocted interpretation of faith. In a crazy bid to prove themselves as pious religionists, they even usurp the personal right of one's freedom of religion, freedom of expression and act coercively and violently to impose their own motives in the name of God's will.

From Mansur Hallaj in Iraq to Sarmad Shaheed in India to Lal Shahbaz Qalandar in Pakistan, most of the Sufi Mystics and Divine Lovers were fearless in their path of love. But their fate was fatal. History, deplorably enough, is replete with their bloodshed. It is common knowledge that Sufi mystics were choked to death in almost every age of Islam and in every Muslim country. Sufis in Arabia, Syria, Iraq and in various parts of the African Muslim region were persecuted for their alleged 'deviation' (Inhiraf) from the 'puritan' Islamic beliefs. For instance—in Iraq, the brutal killing of the Persian Sufi mystic and poet, Mansur Hallaj in 922 was justified for his stating "anal Haqq" (I am the truth)—the allegorical and esoteric words that he spelled out in a spiritual state of *Fana* (salvation). The theological jurists of Baghdad considered this Muslim mystic as a heretic deserving of death penalty.

Another Persian Sufi mystic Ayn al-Qudat Hamadani was executed in 1131 by the *mullahs* of Seljuks. In 1191, the prominent Sufi luminary Shahab-ud-Deen Suhrawardi, the founder of a new Sufi order, was executed by the then Muslim ruler in Syria. In 1417, one of the greatest Sufi masters of Azerbaijan was skinned alive in Syria again.

In 1718, Sufi Shah Inayatullah, who was also an eminent social reformist in Sindh, Pakistan was executed by the Mughal Emperor Yar Muhammad Kalhoro. Deplorably, this nefarious spade of religious violence rocked the history of the Indian subcontinent. In India, Firoz Shah Tughlaq punished the mystic Masood Bakk by a painful death in 1390. More tragically, Mughal king Aurangzeb Alamgeer beheaded the Persian Sufi saint of Jewish origin—Sarmad Kashani, now popularly known as "Sarmad Shaheed", a Sufi martyr in Delhi. He had travelled from Persia to find an abode of peace in India in the 17th century.

In most cases, it was the politically well-established theologians and Islamic jurists who sentenced the Sufis to death on the basis of charges (Fatwas) that considered their writings or sayings heretical. On account of their non-conformist views, such as the notion of Wahdatul Wajud (unity of existence), these Sufis were declared heretics or apostates and sometimes accused of blasphemy. This served as an outright theological justification to slay these Sufi divine lovers and to vandalize their holy shrines later, whenever extremists got an opportunity.

By slaying Sufis and bombing their shrines, extremists have always sought to 'purify' Islam in a bid to restore the 'purity' of the '*Salaf*' (the Islamic predecessors). But in reality, these so-called 'puritanical' Islamists are far removed from the Islam mystically experienced by Prophet Muhammad (pbuh). His traditions set as a classic example of how people of different faiths could peacefully coexist as one nation.

In his state of Madina, all religious communities lived under an alliance of shared values called "Mithaq-e-Madina" (the constitution of Medina), which upheld the immutable clauses of religious pluralism, universal brotherhood and peaceful coexistence.

Not just Muslims, but all non-Muslims living in Madina of the Prophet's times were accorded full protection of life, religious freedom and democratic rights.

One clause in Misaq-e-Madina was stipulated in these words of the Prophet (Hadith):

"I shall dispute with any Muslim who oppresses anyone from among the non-Muslims, or infringes on his right, or puts a responsibility on him which is beyond his capacity or takes something from him against his will." (Reported by Abu Dawood)

Rabi'a's Creed of "Unconditional Love"

The Divine Feminine in Sufi Mysticism

I carry a torch in one hand,

and a bucket of water in the other.

With these things I am going to set Heaven on fire,

So that people can stop praying in fear of Hell.

And see the real goal: Unconditional Love.

~Rabi'a al-Basri (717–801 C.E.) Source: Wikimedia Commons

What Is the Divine Feminine? It is a deeper mystical concept that suggests the existence of a feminine counterpart to the patriarchal and masculine formations of the Divinity. Most practitioners of both Abrahamic and non-Abrahamic faith traditions primarily worship a Masculine God. Rarely do they believe in or show acceptance or tolerance of the Divine Feminine, which forces us to envision God beyond male-chauvinistic theological constructs.

However, the mystical traditions within these religions perceive the Divine Feminine as an essence and energy that complements masculine energy rather than contradicts or conflicts with it. It is meant to harmonise and balance the two. Deeply connected to creativity and imaginative expression, the Divine Feminine allows one to express devotion in his/her fullest potential through a creatively imaginative spiritual quest. For example — in Hindu mythology, "Shakti" refers to the "powerful divine feminine", the active dimension of the Divine Majesty. In contrast, the life and teachings of Hazrat Rabia Basriyya, the famed female Sufi mystic in Islam, exemplify this concept within an Islamic framework. She 'powerfully' and strongly declared her intense and unconditional love for Allah without any 'fear' or hesitation. Rabia coined the idea of "Unconditional Love" and transcended fear and hatred. When asked, "How much do you hate Satan because you love God so much?" she replied, "My heart is so filled with love for God that I find no space in my heart to hate Satan!"

Rabia's existence within Islamic mysticism suggests that there is ample room for the Divine Feminine in Islam or Sufism, even if it is not in mainstream Islam and its conventional schools of thought. Beyond feminine descriptions, Qur'anic references also substantiate this interesting point. For instance, the very first verse of the Qur'an, in the first chapter called Surah Al-Fatiha – also known as Ummul Kitab (Mother of the holy book) – introduces us to the Divine Feminine in Islamic terms.

In Arabic, the wording of this verse is significant: *"In the Name of Allah—the Most Tenderly Compassionate (Ar-Rahman), and the Most Merciful (Ar-Raheem)" (1:1)*.

Significantly, these two Arabic words, which are part of the 99 Divine Names of Allah, hold an even deeper feminine divinity as they derive from the three root letters "r-h-m." The word "rahm" in Arabic means: an embryo or "womb of a mother" denoting deep compassion, care and mercy in Allah's Essence (*Dhaat*) as well as in His Attributes (*Sifaat*). The womb – a divine gift for women to nurture life – is a beautiful representation of a feminine divine that loves, nurtures and cares for us. This lays the foundation for Divine Feminine in Islam and shapes how Muslims should imagine Allah as the Most Merciful and the Most Compassionate (*Rahman* and *Raheem*), whose mercy is like that of a 'tenderly loving mother.' Thus, *Rahman* and *Raheem* are, in essence, feminine attributes of Allah, in contrast to His masculine attributes such as *Qahhar* (the All-Powerful or All-Prevailing) and *Jabbar* (the All-Compelling).

Before I proceed, let me first complete and share the story of Rabia Basriyya. She strongly believed and preached that it is not the fear of Hell that should bring one to devotion or surrender to Allah, but only unconditional and infinite love. She expressed this belief beautifully in her Arabic verses, as translated below:

"I carry a torch in one hand and a bucket of water in the other: with these things I am going to set fire to heaven and put out the flames of hell; so that people will not worship God for want of Heaven or fear of Hell, but simply out of Love."

From time immemorial, there have been two different paths in the world—Love and Fear. While one tells us that the Divine path is all about love and forgiveness, the other overlooks the limitless divine mercy and hope for salvation (Rahma and Rija'a) and creates only fear (Khauf) in human hearts. The Divine Feminine in Sufism teaches us that divine love should be seen as infinite, all-inclusive, and all-encompassing – not as a retrogressive concept espoused by most 'organised religions'. It exhorts us to follow the example and spiritual principles of Rabia Al-Adawiyya Al-Basriyya as a proponent of the basic tenet of Unconditional Love within the Islamic Divine Feminine. Although the clergy – who claim God's love for His creations is restricted – may never reconcile with this idea, the Divine Feminine shows a wider embrace of God's love for all. Not a single creature is exempt from God's bountiful grace and divine mercy (*rahmah*), just as a mother's love knows no bounds or boundaries.

The Holy Prophet himself practised this unconditional divine love and clearly stated, "When God created His creatures, He wrote in His book: "Verily, My mercy (Rahmah) prevails over My wrath" (Sahih al-Bukhari: 3194).

Once, the Holy Prophet (pbuh) and his companions saw a mother bird feeding worms to her babies in a nest. Her actions were so loving, tender, and gentle that the companions were moved by her natural display of love. This beautiful and fascinating scene reminded the Prophet of infinite love and mercy of Allah for humankind. Smiling, he asked his companions, "Are you surprised at the love this mother bird shows to her babies? Let me tell you that God loves you 70 times more than this mother!" This Hadith clearly shows how the Prophet (pbuh) likened Allah's love for His creations to the love of over 70 mothers for their children, thereby recognising and approving the Divine Feminine as an Islamic tradition.

According to another Hadith, Allah divided His mercy into 100 parts, keeping 99 parts with Himself and sent only one part down from heaven to earth. If Allah has unveiled only one per cent of His infinite mercy, imagine the scope of His complete mercy. Through this one percent of His mercy, all creatures – human beings and animals alike – treat one another with compassion. An animal, for instance, lifts its hoof over its child to avoid hurting it. From women to female animals who love, nurture, and care for their babies with loving tenderness, there are innumerable instances of pure, selfless, inherent, and innate love reflecting divine love and infinite mercy of God.

Thus, the Divine Feminine exists in Islamic terms, though it is seldom expressed as it should be. I was first introduced to this concept when I was only a 14-year-old madrasa student. In those early days, in my madrasa, I often wondered why Allah was only referred to as "He" and not "She." This question intrigued me more when I first encountered an Arabic adage about Allah: "Al-ilahu La Yuzakkaru Wa La Yua'annasu" – meaning, the Arabic word *ilaah* (the Divine) is neither masculine nor feminine. This challenged my understanding and raised a straightforward critical question: Why do Muslims exclusively use masculine pronouns and attributes for Allah?

It was only when I deepened my understanding of divinity (İlahiyat) through the rich and imaginative Sufi tradition that I came to see the Divine feminine in Islam. In essence, it has always existed, but it is rarely recognised by the clergymen. Today, the majority of Muslims world over refer to Allah as the masculine "Huwa" in Arabic and "He" in English. With the exception of a few female Muslim scholars such as Professor Sa'diyya Shaikh, Amina Wadud, and Asra Nomani – who exerted concerted efforts and led campaigns to shift the modern Muslim narrative towards a genderless God – you will hardly find an established Islamic authority addressing this in a candid and critical manner.

However, some Sufi philosophers, including the proponent of the Unity of Existence in Islam, Sheikh-e-Akbar Muhyiuddin Ibn-ul-Arabi, have incorporated the Divine Feminine into their mystical discourses. Ibn ul Arabi writes: "… one finds a distinctive and powerful poetics of creation, nurture, power, and spirituality that weaves together the earth, maternity, femininity, women, and the Divine Feminine." He links the earth to the divine, explicitly and unequivocally, as the creative, benevolent, maternal source of the good… He also brings into focus women's procreative capacities and the Divine Feminine, and further states:

"(The earth) gives all of the benefits from her essence (dhāt) and is the location (maḥall) of all good. Thus she is the most powerful (a'azz) of the bodies… She is the patient (ṣabūr), the receptive one (qābila), the immutable one, the firm one…Whenever she moves from fearful awe of God, God secures her by the means of (mountains as) anchors… it is the mother from whom we come, and to whom we return. From her we will come forth once again. To her we are submitted and entrusted. She is the most subtle of foundations (arkān) in meaning. She accepts density, darkness, and hardness only in order to conceal the treasures that God has entrusted to it"… by interweaving maternal, earthy, and generative qualities with the majestic attributes of strength, power, and immutability, Ibn Arabi urges an integration and balance of what might be traditionally categorized as "masculine" and "feminine" attributes within the divine. (*Between the divine and sacred: Islam's forgotten femininity, Elizabeth Arif-Fear*)

Regrettably, those who would ostensibly reject the idea of Divine Feminine in Islam are the self-imposed preachers and so-called believers, but not the lovers of God, who are only obsessed with the "fear of God." They are entirely engaged in spreading this fear, so much so that Allah's

Wrath (*Ghazab*) is highlighted and given primacy in their discourses, and His Mercy (*Rahmat*) is missed out.

This fearful and patriarchal notion of God helps those who commit 'ungodly acts' in the name of God and those who appoint themselves as false 'gods' on earth. Therefore, they forcibly impose their fear, ideology, and religio-political power in the name of establishing "God's will" on various territories around the world. In a crazy bid to maintain and perpetuate their power, they merely showcase their religiosity, and often usurp one's divinely gifted basic human rights and spiritual freedoms: freedom of conscience, freedom of faith, and freedom of expression.

All this continues today in Islam and other religions at the hands of political and religious establishments to pursue their ulterior ambitions for political power.

Ishq-e-Rasool
The Deep Divine Love

Unconditional love for the Prophet and all his loved ones is reckoned as the foundation for Divine Love in Sufism. This devotion to the Prophet is called "Ishq-e-Rasool," which is the basic creed for all Sufi mystics...

Tomb of Prophet Muhammad (pbuh) in Madina Munawwara

Devotion to Prophets is one of the basic creeds of Islamic faith, and infinite, unconditional love for Prophet Muhammad (pbuh) is the pillar of one's belief in his Risalat (prophethood). Significantly, just as *Tawheed* (oneness of

God) is the basic tenet, Ishq-e-Rasool (love and loyalty for the Prophet) is the cornerstone of Islam. For this reason, Muslims of all denominations hold the holy Prophet (pbuh) in the highest esteem.

This reverence can be deeply felt in an Urdu couplet by the poet-philosopher Allama Iqbal, from his celebrated *Jawab-e-Shikwa*:

Ki Mohammed Se Wafa Tune, To Hum Tere Hain

Yeh Jahan Kya Cheez Hai Loh-O-Qalam Tere Hain

Translation: We are yours only with your loyalty towards Prophet Muhammad. Let alone this universe, even the tablet and the pen are yours.

In fact, veneration for the Prophet's holiness is regarded as the foundation of Islamic mysticism (Tasawwuf). Jalaluddin Rumi, the renowned Sufi poet, was so engrossed in unconditional love for the Prophet that he saw him in a pious dream and said: "There has never been a beauty like that of Prophet Muhammad in this world or the next. May the glory of God help him!"

Rumi devoted his entire masterpiece, the *Masnavi* – often called "the second Qur'an" or the "Persian Qur'an" – to the exaltation of the Prophet (pbuh). He writes in Persian:

"I bring blessings upon you, (O Muhammad), so that the breeze of proximity (to God) may increase. Since, with nearness of the whole, all parts are allowed to approach."

Another Persian Sufi poet, Jaami, who wrote extensively mystical literature, was so deeply in love with the Prophet that he composed deeply moving poems for his holiness to comfort his heartache. One such poem reads:

"My soul is breaking into pieces in your separation,

And my heart is becoming weak due to my sins, O Prophet.

I am drowned in your love, and the chain of your love binds my heart.

Yet I don't know this language of love, O Prophet."

This profound degree of love for the Prophet, which is an integral part of the divine path, is enunciated in the Qur'an:

"Say, (O Muhammad), if you should love Allah, then follow me, (so) Allah will love you and forgive you your sins. And Allah is forgiving and merciful." (3:31)

Thus, the Qur'an categorically asked the Prophet to enjoin his companions in the maximum exaltation, love and respect for his holiness, even cautioning them to the extent of not even raising their voices above his voice, as mentioned in another verse (49: 2). Yet the truest expression of this love is to emulate the beloved as an example for all aspects of life.

Rumi says: "If Muhammad does not make a path in our hearts, He does not exist in our hearts." The best part to emulate from the Prophet's life is truthfulness, trustworthiness, and tenderness. Jaami writes in Persian:

Gul az rukhat aamokhta nazuk badani ra badani ra,

Bulbul ze tu aamokhta shireen sukhani ra, sukhani ra.

Translation: Flower has learnt tender-being from your face,

And nightingale has learnt the sweet words from you.

The Mystic of Mehrauli
Martyr of Divine Love

"Those who are shot dead with the dagger of surrender and pleasure are reborn in the unseen."

~Khwaja Qutbuddin Bakhtiyar Kaki

Dargah Khwaja Qutubuddin Bakhtiyar Kaki, Mehrauli Sharif, Delhi

Popularly known as Qutb Saheb, he was the spiritual and intellectual successor of Khwaja Gharib Nawaz Moinuddin Chishti of Ajmer. In fact, the great mystic himself gave him the epithet of the "Qutb," which means "pole" in Arabic and refers to the head of a regional hierarchy in Sufism.

Not many know that Delhi is also the spiritual capital of Indian Sufi mystics and is historically revered among the

South Asian Sufis as "Bais Khwajaaon ki Chaukhat" (the city of the 22 most prominent saints). Delhi's most prominent Muslim mystic of the Chishti Sufi order was Hazrat Khwaja Qutbuddin Bakhtiar Kaki, who emerged as one the major proponents of Wahdatul Wajud (unity of existence) in India, a philosophy closely aligned with the Vedic notion of Advaita or non-dualism.

Qutb Saheb is particularly known for two reasons: his close personal relationship with the divine and mankind, and his mystical worship. Most of his devotional practices remained unknown to the external world, as he never liked to display his spiritual engagements. In fact, worshipping Allah in secret and solitude is the essence of Sufism. Therefore, this mystic of Mehrauli Sharif, is also called Qutb-ul-Aqtab (the greatest Qutb) in India, much like Moinuddin Chishti is revered as the greatest Khwaja (Khwaja-e-Khwajagan).

When the young, sincere seeker Kaki fell at the feet of the great spiritual master and benefactor Khwaja Gharib Nawaz, he was affectionately embraced, blessed and thus enlightened. Raised in Khwaja's disciple-hood, Kaki was taught: "Never turn your face from the light of truth and prove yourself to be a brave man in the Divine path."

After Khwaja Gharib Nawaz's demise, Kaki became the head of the Chishti Sufi order in the subcontinent and carried forward his legacy with complete devotion. Baba Fareeduddin Ganj Shakar, one of his most beloved disciples and direct spiritual successors, played a pivotal role in spreading his teachings. Despite the hostility the Chishti saints faced during the reign of Sultan Shamsuddin Iltutmish, both Bakhtiyar Kaki and Baba Farid continue to be deeply endeared by Muslims and non-Muslims alike.

Even our Father of the Nation, Mahatma Gandhi, credited Khwaja Qutubuddin Bakhtiyar Kaki as one of the key influences on his spiritual thoughts. On January 27, 1948, Gandhiji delivered his last public address at the Mehrauli shrine of Bakhtiyar Kaki. The late Khushwant Singh recounts it in his book, The Novel:

"Gandhi bows to Kaki's tomb. The Musalmans accompanying him requested to utter al-Fateha. So the Mahatma raises his hand and recites: In the name of Allah the beneficent and the merciful." Just as, in his early life, he sought refuge in the discourses of Shrimad Rajchandra as his guide in moments of "spiritual crisis," in his final moments – only three days before his martyrdom – Gandhiji turned to the tomb of Kaki. He would often recite the Sufi poet Ahmad Jaan's following couplet:

"Those who are shot dead with the dagger of surrender and pleasure are reborn in the unseen."

In fact, Khwaja Qutbuddin Bakhtiar Kaki was amongst the pioneers of the Chishti Sufi order in the Indian subcontinent. He is also known as *Qutub-ul-Aqtab* (Pole of the Poles) and *Malik-ul-Mashaikh* (head of the Sufi saints). As the the dearest disciple and spiritual successor of Hazrat Khwaja Gharib Nawaz Moinuddin Chishti, young Qutbuddin fell at the feet of Chishti, and was embraced by him affectionately. He was blessed and raised in a spiritual and humane environment.

It was the era of Sultan Shamsuddin Iltutmish when Bakhtiyar Kaki succeeded Khwaja Gharib Nawaz as the head of the Chishti Sufi order and upheld his legacy with unwavering devotion. His most famous disciple and spiritual successor, Baba Fareed, is deeply endeared by both Muslims and non-Muslims. His discourses and practices enabled his companions to transcend the barriers of caste, creed, colour, region, and race making him a spiritual mentor for humanity at large. During his time, there was no room for divisive forces.

The "Mahbub-e-Elahi"
Beloved of the Divine

Dargah Hazrat Nizamuddin Auliya Mahbub-e-Elahi, Delhi

Popularly known as Mahbub-e-Elahi (beloved of the divine), Hazrat Nizamuddin Auliya was born in 1325. He emerged a pioneer of the Chishti tradition in Delhi which spread widely in the Indian subcontinent. Ziauddin Barani, an eminent historiographer of the 14th century who chose to be a disciple of the saint, notes his overwhelming influence on the religious, social and psychological life of his times. At a time when people were discriminated against irrationally, Mahbub-e-Elahi empowered them to transcend all distinctions of faith, caste, creed and race. This strikingly reflected in the legacy and poetry of his closest disciples, like Amir Khusrau, who said in Persian:

Kafir-e-ishqam musalmani mura darkaar neest;

Har rag-e man taar gashta hajat-e zunnaar neest.

Translation: I am a pagan in my worship of love; I do not need the creed (of Muslims). Every vein of mine has become taunt like a wire, I do not need the (Hindu) girdle.

For Mahbub-e-ilahi, Ishq-e-ilahi (true love for the Divine) was translated into Khidmat-e-Khalq, a sincere service to humanity at large. The surest way to attain personal relationship with Allah (Wisal-e-ilahi), in his view, is to render selfless social service in a manner that one realises that there is no 'I'. There is only the Divine. This realisation attains its perfection at the time of death which is celebrated as Urs (Divine Wedding).

The Chishti tradition of Hazrat Nizamuddin Aulia was strengthened in Delhi at a time when sultans like Muhammad bin Tughlaq were belligerent towards Sufi saints. But several officials of the sultan still became disciples of the then Chishti master, Khwaja Naseeruddin Chiragh Dehlvi, himself a disciple of Hazrat Nizamuddin Aulia. In his exhortation to his disciples, Khwaja would often relay this Persian couplet:

Muraad-e-Ahl-e-Tariqat Libaas-e-Zaahir Neest,

Kamar Ba Khidmat-e-Sultan Be-band-o-Sufi Baash!

Translation: Divine lovers don't aim to attract admiration. They remain a Sufi who serves mankind, even while being in the service of a king.

This divine realisation of the ultimate union with God (*wisal*) as a reward of *khidmat-e-khalq* (service to mankind) is celebrated at the times of Urs at his Dargah through

Qawwalis, Zikr and recitals of Sufi verses (Kalam) composed by his closest disciple Hazrat Amir Khusro Dehlvi.

Khusro's Creed of Divine Love

Amir Khusro, a prominent Sufi mystic, Persian and Hindawi poet, and a Chishti saint, was originally named Abul Hasan Ameenuddin Dehlvi. Known as "Tuti-e-Hind" (the parrot of India), he was a proponent of universal mysticism and higher spiritual consciousness in Indian Chishti-Sufi tradition.

Initially, Khusro's poetry was not deeply imbued with mysticism during his service to seven Sultans of the Delhi Sultanate, including Sultan Allauddin Khilji, until he met his Sufi master, Hazrat Nizamuddin Auiya. He transformed his inner world, which created a tremendous spiritual urge in his heart and poetry.

Khusro strengthened the foundational principles of the Chishti Sufi order, such as the two key precepts of "Khidmat-e-Khalq" (service to mankind) and "Sulh-e-Kul" (reconciliation with all)—as taught by Hazrat Khwaja Nizamuddin Aulia and originally conceived by Hazrat Khwaja Gharib Nawaz Moinuddin Chishti, the founder of Chishti Order in India. Many of his Hindawi, Persian and Avadhi Kalaams (verses) focused on an inclusivist and pluralist tradition emanating from the universal essence of Wahdat-ul-Wujud – Unity of the Existence.

As the concept of "Urs" connotes divine union of the saint with his Most Beloved, Khusro attained *Wisal-e-ilahi* (union with the Divine) alongside his Divine Beloved (*Mahbub-e-ilahi*) Hazrat Nizamuddin Aulia RA.

Born in 653 AH, Khusro was initially not mystically-inclined during his poetic career at the *Shahi Darbars* (royal courts), where he served seven Sultans of the Delhi

Sultanate, including Sultan Allauddin Khilji (1296-1316). However, his encounter with Hazrat Nizamuddin Auliya, transformed his inner world, creating a profound mystical inclination and tremendous spiritual transformation that became the essence of his poetry, and later became his dearest disciple.

This deep spiritual relationship between a Murshid (master) and Murid (seeker) fostered a beautiful synthesis of mystical oneness, spiritual unity, and harmony within the Indian Sufi tradition. This is beautifully reflected, and experienced in many of the Avadhi and Farsi verses of Amir Khusro:

Khusro raen suhaag ki, jaagi pi ke sung,

Tun mero mun pi-u ko, dovu bhaye ek rung.

Translation: Khusrau, the bride, spends the eve of her wedding awake with her beloved (in such a way that),

The body belongs to her, but heart to the beloved, The two become one.

Amir Khusro also strengthened the bedrock of harmonious and humane values ingrained in the ancient Indian philosophy of Vasudhaiva Kutumbakam (the world is one family). This was proclaimed as the basic premise of Amir Khusro's poetry and philosophy, and was captured in one of his Persian couplets:

"Almighty holds dear those who love Him for the sake of human beings, and those who love human beings for the sake of Almighty."

If we delve deeper into the meaning behind Khusro's Persian poetry, including masnawis and Hindawi dohas, he emphasises the Sufi notion of Wahdatul Wajud (Unity of the Being), which is closely aligned with the Vedantic concept of Advaita (non-dualism). Many of Khusro's

Hindawi, Persian, and Avadhi kalaams (verses) lay a greater emphasis on an inclusivist and pluralist tradition, which emanated from the universal essence of *Wahdat-ul-Wujud*.

Khusro was fluent in Arabic, Persian, Turkish, Sanskrit and other languages, however he chose to express his spiritual experiences and unity in indigenous poetic styles, using Hindawi Kalaam, Avadhi, Khari Boli, and Brij Bhasha. His dohas, alongside Persian poetry like Rub'aee and masnavis (rhymed pairs) – like Jalaluddin Rumi's world-famed Persian collection Masnavi-i-Ma'navi– which is considered the second Qur'an in Sufism—Khusro's kalaams are replete with anecdotes and stories derived from the Qur'anic wisdom, prophetic traditions, and the tales of early Sufi sages. Significantly, he composed a large part of his work to illustrate a crucial point; India's sanctity in Islamic tradition and its centrality in universal spirituality, and each aspect of it is explained in detail in his Dohas.

It is a common knowledge that the saddest part of Khusro's life came after the demise of his Murshid Hazrat Nizamuddin Aulia. Even his own death was nothing as compared to his Murshid's. Bereaved Khusro, in an extreme pain of separation from his most beloved, painted his pain in a lyrical miniature:

Gori sove sej par, Mukh par daley kes;

Chal Khusrau ghar aapnay, saanjh bhaee chahu desh.

Translation: The fair maiden rests on a bed of roses, Her face covered with a lock of hair; Come Khusrau let's go home now, darkness settles on the world now.

As per the will of his Hazrat Nizamuddin Aulia, Khusro was never allowed to come close to his grave, as he feared that his body would forget the laws of the mortal world and break open the grave to embrace his closest disciple. But then after his death, Khusro was buried just next to Hazrat Nizamuddin. Today, every visitor to Hazrat Nizamuddin Aulia's shrine has to first pay obeisance to the grave of Hazrat Amir Khusro in order to complete his or her Ziyarat. His death anniversary which is known as *Urs-e-Khusrawi* or the "Divine Wedding of Amir Khusro" begins from the 16th Shawwal six months after Hazrat Nizamuddin's Urs. As "Urs" in Sufism connotes the divine union of the saint with his most beloved, Khusro attained *Wisal-e-ilahi* (union with the Divine) with the Divine Beloved (*Mahbub-e-ilahi*) Hazrat Nizamuddin Aulia RA in a divine play of love, as he beautifully sang before his death:

Khusro baazi prem ki, main kheli pi ke sang,

Jeet gayi to prya mere, haari to pi ke sang

Translation: I play the game of love with my beloved. If I win he is mine. And even if I lose, I'm his.

"Eid-e-Gulabi"
A Sufi Celebration of Colours!

There are different ways to celebrate colours in India. The festival of Holi is celebrated across the country in distinct styles. Pilgrims and tourists from abroad flock to Mathura, Vrindavan and Barsana to witness Holi. Be it in the city or village, Indian people celebrate Holi in their special way. The famous Holi of Barsana is well-known today.

But not many are aware that in this multicultural and colourful country, an amazingly unique style of Holi celebration also exists—the Sufi celebration of divine colours—popularly known as "Eid-e-Gulabi." This is the Holi celebrated at dargahs like the holy shrine of the famous Sufi saint Haji Waris Ali Shah, located in Barabanki, UP.

Punjabi Sufi mystic, poet, and revolutionary philosopher Sayyid Abdullah Shah Qadri, more popularly known as Bulleh Shah composed these beautiful couplets:

Hori Khelungi, Keh Bismillah.

Nam Nabi Ki Ratn Chadi,

Boond Padi Allah Allah.

Rang Rangeeli Ohi Khilave,

Jis Seekhi Ho Fanaa Fi Allah.

"Alastu Bi Rabbikum" Pritam Bole,

Sab Sakhiyan Ne Ghunghat Khole.

Qaloo Bala, Yunhi Kar Bole, "La Ilaha Illallah"

Translation:

In the name of Allah, I begin to play Holi reciting Bismillah. Cast like a gem in the name of the holy Prophet (pbuh).

Each drop falls with the beat of Allah, Allah. Only he may play with these colourful dyes, who has learnt to lose himself in Allah.

"Am I not your lord?" asked the lover.

And all maids lifted their veils.

Everyone said, "Yes!" and repeated: "There's only one God."

Bulleh Shah rendered these mystically nuanced poetic exhortations of divine love and ultimate union during his celebration of Holi in an undivided India (1680-1757). His words, however, remain profoundly relevant today in the conflict-ridden and communally sensitive society of the Indian subcontinent.

Munshi Zakaullah, in his book "Tareekh-e-Hindustani," has rightly asked: "Who says Holi is just a Hindu festival?" The last Mughal Emperor, Bahadur Shah Zafar, a Sufi follower, would rejoice in Holi's celebration. He believed his religion would not be affected by this cultural celebration and even encouraged his Hindu ministers to smear his forehead with gulal on Holi. He expressed his adoration for the festival in his poetry:

Kyun Mope Maari Rang Ki Pichkaari

Dekh Kunwarji Dungi Main Gaari

Bhaag Sakun Main Kaise Moso Bhaago Nahin Jaat

Thaande Ab Dekhun Main Baako Kaun Jo Sun Mukh Aat

Bahut Dinan Mein Haath Lage Ho Kaise Jaane Deoon

Aaj Main Phagwa Ta Sau Kanha Faita Pakad Kar Leoon.

Translation:

"Why have you squirted me with colour? O Kunwarji, I will swear at you. I can't run. I am unable to run.

I am now standing here and want to see who can drench me. After many days have I got my hands on you; how can I let you go? I will catch you by your cummerbund and play Holi with you."

At the Indian Sufi shrines like Dewa Sharif, the dargah of Haji Waris Ali Shah in Uttar Pradesh, Holi has been celebrated with as much enthusiasm as Eid ul-Fitr. Thus, it is popularly known as Eid-e-Gulabi or "Pink Eid" in the age-old Sufi tradition. Waris Ali Shah, more popularly known as Sarkar Waris Piya of Dewa Sharif, was an inclusivist Indian Muslim mystic from Barabanki.

Besides an array of beautiful spiritual traits, Dewa Sharif is India's most notable Dargah today where Holi is celebrated as "Eid-e-Gulabi" with a similar fervour as in Hindu faith traditions. Each year during the colourful festival of Holi, , the shrine visitors at Dewa Sharif invoke the divine blessings through the Sufi celebration of colours. This is of crucial significance Of Eid-e-Gulabi. Such Sufi festivities are vital to our collective spiritual consciousness in India.

For decades, people have gathered to celebrate the Sufi Holi, known as Eid-e-Gulabi, at the sanctum of Dewa Sharif.

Prof. Wahajuddin Alwi, a relative of Waris Pak's family lineage and the husband of his great granddaughter, Asma Parween, explained to this writer: "Since Waris Piya wanted people in India to transcend religious/sectarian divides, he participated in Hindu festivals like Holi.

The syncretic Sufi celebration of colours in India traces its roots to Hazrat Khwaja Nizamuddin Aulia and his disciple, Hazrat Amir Khusro. They revered colours, especially "pink" and "yellow," as divine expressions. Their mysticism, expressed through deeply moving Sufi discourses and Persian and *Hindavi* poetry, incorporated Holi and Basant into the Dargah celebrations. Hazrat Amir Khusro's couplet on the divine connotations of colours reflects this tradition in his Hindavi Kalam:

Kheluungii Holi, Khaaja Ghar Aaye,

Dhan Dha Bhaaghamare Sajni, Khaaja Aaye Aangan Mere

Translation: I shall play Holi as Khwaja has come home, blessed is my fortune, o friend, as Khwaja has come to my courtyard.

During the Mughal era, especially during the reign of emperors Shahjahan and Jalaluddin Akbar, Holi was celebrated as *Eid-ul-Alwan* (The Colourful Eid) and Eid-e-Gulabi. It was also known as *"Aab-e-Pashi"* (shower of colourful flowers) and is mentioned in *Tuzk-e-Jahangiri*, Nuruddin Muhammad Jahangir's autobiography. Jahangir himself held *Mehfil-e-Holi*.

Sufi Basant: A Symbol of Multicultural Mysticism

The beautiful and historical Sufi tradition of celebrating Basant, which marks the seasonal shift from gloomy winter to joyous spring, is an epoch-making part of Indian Muslim mysticism. It began at the famous Dargah Hazrat Nizamuddin Auliya during the 13th-14th century in Delhi and is still celebrated at major Chishti shrines. Growing up in Delhi, Basant has always had a special appeal to me since childhood. While for our Hindu brethren it is dedicated to Saraswati, a deity of wisdom, music, flowing water, and abundance of knowledge, art, and aesthetics, many Muslims in India have celebrated it as what they have beautifully named "Sufi Basant."

According to Hindu mythology, Saraswati is depicted as a pristine lady seated on a white lotus blooming in a wide stretch of water. She is adorned in dazzling white attire, with white flowers and pearls, and holds a Veena, a stringed Hindustani musical instrument like a sitar, often used for mystical music.

In Sikhism too, Basant Panchami holds a spiritual dimension. "Basant Raga" constitutes an important composition (raag) included in the Guru Granth Sahib and is sung with great reverence. Guru Arjan Dev ji urged people to submit themselves to the true Guru to achieve liberation and ultimate union with the Divine. This essential message of the Basant Panchami was greatly appreciated by the Sufi Mystics, especially Hazrat Nizamuddin Auliya and his closest disciple, Hazrat Ameer

Khusro. Thus, Sufi Basant is celebrated every year at Dargah Hazrat Nizamuddin Auliya, with a beautiful anecdote behind it:

Once, Hazrat Nizamuddin was deeply grieved by the death of his nephew, Khwaja Taqiuddin Nooh, who was very dear to him. As he had no children of his own, he loved his adopted family from his sister's side, very deeply. Overwhelmed by grief of his nephew's demise, he went into an enforced isolation and asked his disciples to stop all activities at the Dargah. This saddened his most beloved mureed, Khusro, who could not bear to see his Murshid (spiritual master) in sorrow, as he spent all his time at his nephew's grave at "Chilla-e-Sharif." Longing to bring joy to his murshid, Khusro devised an ingenious plan.

One day, Khusro saw some Hindu women in yellow *saris* carrying mustard flowers and singing hymns. When he asked the women about their ritual, they explained to him it was to make their deity, Saraswati happy. Inspired, Khusro immediately decided to use this festival to bring a smile back to his murshid's face. He dressed in a yellow sari, carried mustard flowers, and appeared before Hazrat Nizamuddin. Seeing Khusro like this, Hazrat Nizamuddin Auliya, who loved the colour yellow, smiled and felt elated. This marked the end of his mourning. Since then, the beautiful tradition of Sufi Basant has been an integral part of the Khanqah's annual celebrations. On this occasion, Khusro wrote a beautiful poem in Brij Bhasha:

Yellow mustard blossoms have covered entire fields.

The mango tree is in bloom,

The flame of the forest is in bloom,

The Koel bird flits singing from one branch to another,

And the fair lady decks herself

With marigold blossoms the gardener's wife fetches for her.

The season is full of yellow flowers

That we carry to the door of Hazrat Nizamuddin.

Years ago, my lover had promised he would come visit me.

Through this act, Khusro succeeded in lifting his murid's spirits. This gesture of love and the celebration of Basant brought smiles back to Hazrat Nizamuddin and marked the end of his mourning period. Since then, the Dargah continues to celebrate "Sufi Basant" with a joyous procession as it turned the grieved Murshid into an elated one!

Sufi Basant at Dargah Hazrat Nizamuddin Auliya, Delhi

Today, mustard flowers once again brighten the Dargah. Devotees and shrine visitors of Mahbub-e-Ilahi, Hazrat Nizamuddin Auliya, joyously celebrate Sufi Basant. Urdu and Persian Sufi compositions are routinely performed through Qawwalis including Khusro's lovely composition:

Aaj Basant Manaaley Suhagan

Aaj Basant Manaaley Suhagan

Translation:

Rejoice, O my Beloved, rejoice,

It's Basant (spring), rejoice!

On the eve of Sufi Basant, the Daragh is drenched in yellow. Devotees from all walks of life– irrespective of gender, religion, or caste– join the celebration. Amidst the fragrance of yellow flowers and enveloping sounds of Qawwalis, the dargah immerses itself in *"Sama,"* symbolising ecstasy, amity, and the syncretic Sufi culture.

The spiritually-inclined Muslims, Hindus, Sikhs and people of other faiths celebrate Sufi Basant together at the holy shrine of Hazrat Nizamuddin Auliya. Celebrated for over seven centuries, Basant is an enduring symbol of Hindu-Muslim harmony. Festivals and traditions like Basant unite us as a nation across religious, cultural, linguistic, and social divides. Though Basant is not mentioned in any religious scripture — the Qu'ran, the Vedas, or the Bhagavad Gita–it requires a large heart to embrace the notion of love and shared traditions in our collective consciousness. The essence, and cultural and spiritual connotation of Sufi Basant cannot be narrowed down to a particular religion or community.

As the Chishti Sufi adage says: "Your minds have limits but not your hearts, for they are receptacles of endless capacity." This guiding light and mystical wisdom from the Chishti tradition of Indian Sufi saints continue to inspire unity and amity. The famous Urdu poet of Delhi, Rakim Dehlvi, aptly wrote in his couplets:

Khudaya Ba'd e Mahshar Ke Agar Aalam Ho Phir Paida,

Tamashagaah-e-aalam Mein Nizamuddin Shahi ho.

Translation: O God! After the day of resurrection, if the world comes back to life,

Give the crown to Hazrat Nizamuddin Auliya in the circus of this world.

Music & Mysticism— Makhdoom e Simnan & Sufi Sima'a

A Sufi Discourse of Makhdoom Ashraf Jahangir Simnani

The tomb of Makhdoom Ashraf Jahangir Simnani in Kichaucha

Mindless violence has been perpetrated against Muslim musicians, singers, and many other artists by radical Islamists and extremists on theological grounds. In so-called Islamic countries like Pakistan, Sufi musicians and famous Qawwals, such as Amjad Sabri, have been murdered for singing devotional songs. The gruesome killing of prominent Pakistani Qawwal Amjad Sabri in June, 2016 was not the first case of silencing Sufi singers. To date, around two dozen Muslim musicians, singers, and artists have been killed across the country.

In India, it is not so easy to kill an artist on theological grounds. However, Fatwas against music and musicians, especially Sufi singers, have also been issued in India without fearing the law.For instance, in Assam in 2017, around 40 Ulema unanimously issued a decree against 16-year-old singer Nahid Afreen for singing devotional songs. In Mumbai, Raza Academy, a political outfit of the Barelwi School of Thought, issued a fatwa against music maestro A.R. Rahman who composed music, even in good faith, for the Iranian film *Muhammad: The Messenger*, directed by Majid Majidi. Deobandi Ulema have also been at the forefront of issuing fatwas against music, including devotional songs. Last year, some of them issued a Fatwa against a YouTuber and female Muslim singer, Farmani Naaz, a resident of Muzaffarnagar, Uttar Pradesh. While many Indian Muslims and Hindus praised her for beautifully singing a devotional Hindi poem with a non-stereotypical approach, some Deobandi Ulema called for boycotting her from the community.

Against this backdrop, revisiting and reading the Sufi discourse on music and musical instruments, with a special reference to Sufi music known as *Sima'a* is pertinent. An objective probe into the Islamic literature on this subject reveals that both promoters and opponents of Sufi *Sima'a*– in the past and even now– have often indulged in exaggeration. Generally, anti-music Islamic theologians lack the intellectual and spiritual capacity to understand the Sufi discourses on music and *Sima'a*. Therefore, I have chosen to study an authentic Sufi perspective on music from the viewpoint of the Chishti-Sufi saint and theologian, Makhdoom Ashraf Jahangir Simnani.

Among the most notable Chishti Sufi masters of India, Makhdoom Ashraf Jahangir Simnani Noor Bakshi (RA) shines as bright as the sun and the moon on the spiritual horizon. In the spiritual realm, his stature and persona with his magnificent work and magnanimous character, coupled with his unceasing grace and blessings, continue to attract and inspire masses. He belonged to a noble family historically regarded as a cradle of divine wisdom (*Marifat*), spiritual intellect, and gnosis or Haqiqat (knowledge of spiritual realities). Moreover, Faizabad in Uttar Pradesh, where the Khanqah-e-Ashrafia is located, has been a great abode of Sufi scholars, Urdu poets, and Ulema.

From the Ashrafiya family, in every era, great personalities of grace and perfection. with eminence, immense local popularity, cultural connections and a wider embrace for indigenous people and universal values emerged, benefiting all.

Their 'scholarly Sufism' and various other achievements in different lawful pursuits, have lit lamps of wisdom and knowledge during their time, enlightening the world with their rays today. One such spiritual luminary was Hazrat Syed Shah Abu Ahmad Ali Hussain Ashraf Ashrafi Mian Al-Hasani Al-Hussaini Al-Jilani (RA). A disciple of his elder brother, Qutb ul-Mushaikh, Hazrat Shah Ashraf Hussain, he received spiritual authority *(Ijazat* and *Khilafat)* after completing *Suluk* (treading the spiritual path). In addition, the alchemy of close companionship with dozens of Masters and *Mashaikh* made him a master of various chains of Sufism combining *Ma'rifat, Haqiqat* and *Tariqat.* He combined the blessings of seventeen *Sufi Silsilas* (chains), becoming a repository of the collective grace of Indian Sufi masters.

Makhdoom Simnani: A Brief Introduction

Following in the footsteps of Khwaja Moinuddin Chishti (RA), the most celebrated Chishti Sufi saint of India, Hazrat Sayed Ashraf Jahangir Simnani (1287 – 1386 CE) left his birthplace, Simnan in Iran, and settled in India. Revered by both Indian Hindus and Muslims, Makhdoom Simnani, popularly known as *"Makhdoom-e-Paak,"* was an eminent saint of the Chishti and Qadiri orders. He was the chief disciple of Hazrat Alaul Haq Pandavi, a generous Sufi sage of Bengal, and a disciple of the renowned Chishti master, Hazrat Akhi Siraj Aaina-e-Hind.

Makhdoom-e-Paak established his own Sufi order (*Silsila*) through his spiritual disciple Syed Shah Abdur Razzaq Nurul-Ain, the 11th direct descendant of the renowned Sufi Sheikh Abdul Qadir Jilani (RA), the founder of the Qadiriyya Order. His shrine, "Aastana-e-Hazrat Jahangir Simnani," remains a revered a Sufi hospice. .

The Persian-origin Indian Sufi mystics fervently taught and promoted global peace, inclusive spirituality, and non-violence. Their shrines continue to attract people of all faiths. In today's climate of religious disharmony, communal hatred, and faith-inspired extremism, Indian Sufi saints of Persian remaine beacons of hope, light, and guidance. They enriched India's mystical traditions, emphasising brotherhood of mankind, inclusivity, and religious pluralism. This was key behind the vast popularity of Sufi sages in the country.

The Teachings and Traditions

Makhdoom Ashraf Jahangir Simnani's teachings, as outlined in his Sufi discourse *"Lataif-e-Ashrafi,"* continue to serve as a guiding light.. His work delves deeply into two fundamental tenets of Islamic spiritual wisdom: *Wahdat-e-Khudawandi* (Unity of the Divine or Oneness of God) and

Wahdat-e-Insani (Unity of mankind). He was the first to introduce Wahdat as a deeply nuanced and expansive notion of love. *"Wahdat* means annihilation of the lover in the characteristics of their beloved," he stated.

Remarkably, Makhdoom Ashraf detailed five causes of love and classified different categories of lovers. In the chapter titled "Teachings and Instructions" (*Ta'aleemat o Irshadaat*), he articulated rare and precious sayings in Persian that, when reflected upon, evoke a sense of spiritual sweetness and unwavering faith in the divine. You will bear witness of being intoxicated by the unseen divine intervention.

These teachings, concise yet profound, encapsulate vast and valuable concepts. A few notable concepts include:

(1) "May Allah forbid it! Never be miserly, for miserliness is a characteristic of disbelievers. The clearest proof of their miserliness is that it is easier for them to dig a mountain with their nails than to bring the *Kalima* to their tongue." (Lataif e Ashrafi, p. 177).

(2) "Adorning one's limbs with good acts of worship and beautifying one's inner self with desirable virtues are the source of divine grace and endless blessings."

(3) "Fasting is better than all acts of worship because it includes austerity, struggle, observation, generosity, dignity, and enlightenment. Both spiritually and physically, it awakens the heart, arising with insomnia."

Theological Views on Music

Notably, Syed Ashraf Jahangir Simnani (RA) was not just a spiritual luminary known as "Huzoor Ghosul Alam" (the benefactor of the world) but also an influential Islamic theologian. He popularised *Wahdat-e-Imani* (oneness in belief), *Wahdat-e-Ilmi* (oneness in knowledge) and *Wahdat-*

e-Hali (oneness in spiritual condition) with robust theological reasoning.

In his special discourse on Sufi music, or Sima'a, encapsulated in the 20th chapter of "Lataif-e-Ashrafi," he says: "When Divine lovers and seekers listen to the sound of musical instruments—chords, strings, harps and the Ney (an end-blown flute used in Persian, Turkish and Arabic music) – their memories are transported back to their real homeland, and their hearts are illuminated by the light and love of God."

Although Makhdoom Simnani acknowledges that Sima'a is a contentious issue in Islamic jurisprudence, he accords it theological legitimacy for those with a natural affinity for music, provided it is pursued lawfully. Citing extensively quoted from the Qur'an, the Sunnah, the sayings of the *Sahaba* (Prophet's companions) and the Companions (*Taba'een*), as well as the established views of prominent Imams and Ulemas, he infers that singing, dancing, playing drums or the Duff (Middle Eastern musical instrument), and holding a *Mehfil-e-Sima'a* (Sufi musical gathering) is not forbidden in Islam.

"All of this is allowed and their permissibility is substantiated by the traditions and sayings of Hanafi scholars and jurists," he explains. In this regard, Makhdoom Simnani quotes Imam Abu Yusuf and Imam Muhammad, the two leading disciples of Imam Abu Hanifa, stating that the fatwa of Imam Abu Hanifa and other earlier rulings forbidding music in Islam, declaring it 'Haram' were context specific, and cannot be generalized. According to him, the prohibition applied to music that o promoted vulgarity and moral corruption, not to music per se (Mutlaq e Ghina).

More importantly, Makhdoom Simnani emphasises the spiritual state of the listener (Saame') in *Sufi Sima'a*. He asserts that anyone listening to Sufi music must view it as an invocation of the divine attributes of Almighty Allah.

Imam Ali, who once remarked upon hearing a melodious voice, "Subhan'Allah! Only Allah the Almighty will last."

Various other interesting points have been made and several authoritative quotations have been cited by Makhdoom Simnani in his Lataif-e-Ashrafi, as detailed in the recently published Urdu book "Music in Islam: A Study of Fiqhi and Sufi Traditions" by Dr Zishan Ahmad Misbahi, senior lecturer in Jamia A'arifia at the Khanqah-e-Arifia, Allahabad, UP. The book has been received reasonably well on this subject and is being seen as a sharp rebuttal to the Ulema and Muftis who indiscriminately issue fatwas against all types of music, especially Sufi music.

In his writings, Makhdoom Simnani also addressed an intellectual query regarding the legitimate use of t drums during Muharram processions (*Azadari* or *T'aziya*). he differentiates between two types of drums: those played merely for amusement, which he deems impermissible (haram), and those used for noble purposes, which he considers permissible (Mashr'u).He elaborates: "The drum (*Naqqara*) played on the battlefield or to announce the march of an army is permissible. Similarly, there is compelling evidence from the holy shrine of Hazrat Ibrahim Khalilullah (pbuh), where drums are routinely played during the distribution of *Langar* (shrine food) notifying all shrine visitors, travelers and neighbours to partake. Even some Mashaikh (Sufi masters) play the drum at the time of their descent. In fact, the drum was also played at the time of distribution of Langar at Hazrat Sheikh Abu Ishaq Ghazrooni's shrine from where this writer (Syed Ashraf Jahangir Simnani) was also allowed to play the drum and was bestowed with special knowledge of it. For the saints and dervishes (*Faqeers*), having food is also a form of worship and any act that leads to worship is legitimate in Islamic Shariah." (Source: Lataif e Ashrafi Urdu, Latifah 19th p. 484, published by Makhdoom Ashraf Academy).

Krishna in Sufi Mysticism
The Prophet of Divine Love

Do you know that some of the Indian Muslim Mystics especially in the Bengal region introduced Prophet Muhammad (pbuh) as Shri Krishna's Avtar in Arabia? Even before them, Mahmud Ghaznavi used the Sanskrit nomenclature 'avatar' for the holy Prophet (pbuh) on the coins minted by him, says Abu Raihan Al-Biruni founder of Indology and the father of 'Comparative Religion' in India. But how many of us actually know it today?

Noted Indian Muslim scholar and Sufi poet, Maulana Syed Fazl-ul-Hasan Hasrat Mohani, who coined the Urdu slogan "Inquilab Zindabad" during the freedom movement used to visit Vrindavan in Mathura before he went to perform his Hajj in Makkah. Have you ever heard of it?

Well, this has been the deeply-seated and historically rooted Muslim Mystical tradition in India—call it Sufism or whatever you like. Some would rather call it 'Krishnite Sufism'. The thrust of this tradition is that like every other nation and people, India too has been blessed with the presence of the holy Prophets and Apostles of Allah (*Paighambars*). Therefore, in all likelihood, the king of Ayodhya Maryada Purshottam Shri Ram, and the Prince of Dwarka Shri Krishna and their Avatars may actually have been the holy prophets sent to the Indian subcontinent and thus their teachings and traditions must be held in high regard by the Indian Muslims. This has been propounded by the authoritative Sufi mystics in India such as the Naqshbandi saint and scholar Mirza Mazhar Jaan-e-Jaan

(1689-1781) and the Chishti Sufi poet of the 18th century, Shah Turab Chishti.

In fact, some Indian Ulema believe Shri Krishna may be one of the Divine Messengers who visited India, based on a hadith narration mentioned in a book called "*Tarikh Hamdan*". According to the history of Hamdan Daylami (Chapter Al-Kaaf), there was a prophet in India whose colour was black and his name was Kahin (the saint).

Long ago, an Indian Muslim mystic popularly known as "*Raskhan*" immersed himself in Krishna consciousness. His deep devotion to Shri Krishna or Krishna-Bhakti culminated in marvellous poetry that he composed in his ecstasy and that is still sung by the common people of Mathura. Today, on the occasion of Janmashtami, many Hindus and Muslims celebrate the birth of Shri Krishna, by reciting his poems and offering prayers for the salvation and protection of all human beings. Indian Muslims remember Shri Krishna on Janmashtami in an effort to revive and rejuvenate their links with the glorious history of the Indo-Muslim mystical tradition.

Khwaja Hasan Nizami, a prominent Sufi scholar of the Chishti Order, popularly known in Urdu as *Musawwir-e-Fitrat* (a natural artist and essayist) who wrote many essays on Indian Sufism, published his book on Shri Krishna titled "*Krishn Beiti*" in 1917 which was later renamed as "*Krishna Katha*" or "*Krishna Jeewan*". In this book, Khwaja Hasan Nizami sought to clear various misconceptions about the persona of Shri Krishna, particularly prevailing among Muslims.

At the very outset, he described Shri Krishna as a great man who taught Indians the secrets of the spiritual and material worlds. The chapter in the book on the blessed birth of Shri Krishna is titled "Dawn of the Truth" in which he writes that after the long dark night, Shri Krishna's birth came as the beacon of hope and light. Much like his contemporary Urdu poet Hafeez Jalandhari, Khwaja Hasan Nizami called Shri Krishna the "light of India". Not just that, he also went on in his book to do an intellectual refutation of the arguments of Arya Samaji scholars like Lala Lajpat Rai who maintain that Sri Krishna was not the incarnation and even the author of the Shrimad Bhagavad Gita. Khwaja Hasan Nizami retorts: "O Indians, do not disrespect your nation in a bid to please foreigners, and give your predecessors their rightful place". Notably, Khwaja Hasan Nizami thus attaches paramount importance to the study of Hinduism, its culture and civilization as an exercise in nation-building.

One of the substantial points that Khwaja Hasan Nizami makes in his book is that the life and teachings of Shri Krishna should not be learned from secondary sources or books written by Western scholars or European authors. Many of the misconceptions about Shri Krishna are either sheer Western propaganda or an outcome of misreading his life. For instance—accusing Shri Krishna of 'nudity' or slandering his polygamy was actually a Western ploy and a distorted colonial narrative that the British wanted to spread to further their ends. Therefore, Khwaja Hasan Nizami, categorically states that such accusations made by the colonialists and their sympathizers were meant to buttress the claim that the native Indians had no civilization, which is actually frivolous and untenable. Thus, this Indian Muslim scholar of the Nizami Sufi Order tried to de-colonize the narratives around the persona of Shri Krishna. He penned this book passionately as a devout Indo-Muslim scholar.

Even before Khwaja Hasan Nizami, Shah Burhanuddin Janam, in his 16th-century work 'Irshad Nama', which had a mystical theme, and *'Sukh Sahela'*, which consisted of his couplets, described the fascinating perceptions of Sri Krishna. To shed light on his greatness and popularity, he proudly stated that Krishna is the one who has sixteen thousand Gopis: *Bal Baram Tu Achari Hai, Sola Sahas Nari Hai*. Hazrat Mahmood Daryai was also a Krishna-Bhakt Sufi mystic and poet. He described himself as the bride and the Divine as the bridegroom in full synergy with the Hindi-style poetry.

Among the mystical Urdu poets, Shri Krishna has always been a beloved (Mahboob). Nazeer Akbarabadi—the 18th-century Urdu poet known as "Father of Nazm"—wrote poems not only on Shri Krishna but also a beautiful poem about Baladevji, Krishna's brother and his Mela. Even Mohsin Kakorvi, the noted Urdu poet famous for his Na'at who composed his *Qasida "Madeeh Khairul Mursaleen"* (in praise of the holiest Prophet) invoked Shri Krishna. Celebrating Prophet Muhammad's birthday (Meelad-un-Nabi), he composed the following couplet:

Simt-e-Kashi Se Chala Janib-e-Mathura Badal

Barq Ke Kandhe Pe Laati Hai Saba Ganga Jal

Translation: The clouds are moving ecstatically from Kashi to Mathura and the sky will remain covered with dense clouds as long as there is Shri Krishna.

Maulana Hasrat Mohani was also one of the Indian Muslim mystics who fervently celebrated divine love and devotion towards Shri Krishna. As described by himself, he was a *'Sufi Mo'min'* (a believing Sufi), and an *Ishtiraaki* Muslim (secular Muslim), *Aashiq-e-Rasool* (lover of the holy Prophet), and at the same time a Krishn-Bhakt (devotee of Krishna).

While Hasrat Mohani composed several Urdu poems (*Na'at*) in praise of Prophet Muhammad (pbuh) and other spiritual invocations (*Munajat*), he also paid beautiful tributes of love and devotion, through his mystic poetry, to Shri Krishna. One on hand, Mohani invoked the holy Prophet as follows:

Khyaal e Yaar Ko Dil Se Mita Do Yaa Rasool Allah

Khird Ko Apna Deewana Bana Do Yaa Rasool Allah

Translation: O Apostle of Allah, purge my heart of all metaphorical love and all worldly thoughts. Draw my attention towards yourself as your devotee, O Apostle of Allah!

On the other hand, Mohani did not forget the earlier prophets who had been sent down to various territories, especially India. An embodiment of compassion, tenderness and divine love, in Maulana Hasrat Mohani's poetry Krishna is greatly revered as "Hazrat Krishna." Some of his moving mystical poems about Shri Krishna in Urdu are as follows:

To Se Lagaai Kanhaai Preet

Kahu Or Kisurati Ab Aai Kaahe

Hasrat Tan Man Dhan Sab Waar-Ke

Mathura Nagar Ramaai Chali Dhooni

Translation: My heart has fallen in love with Kanhaiya. Why would anyone else think of it now? O Hasrat, give up all that is yours for him. Then go to Mathura and become a mystic.

I stand where the deep knowledge and realisation of love is found,

Who is the one whose flute's melody fills me?

Gokul's land also became the beloved of the world,

When I recited the Kalima in the name of his love.

Vrindavan too turned out to be a picture of heaven,

Because of his feet, there is a spring that becomes a harbinger of paradise.

What a good fortune, Hasrat,

Your heart brims with a glowing love for the beauty of Musk!

Bearing in mind the religious fanatics who may scoff at his devotion to Krishna, the devotional Maulana issues an inclusive "fatwa" in justifying his love:

Puna Hoe Na Kipreet Ka Paap Shyam

Kou Kaahe Pashchatap Karat Hai

Neha Ki Aag Maatan-Pupa

Jalat Rahi Chup-Chaap Kab Lag

Translation: Loving Shyam is not a sin, nor a virtue. So why do people repent? How long do I have to burn silently in the fire of love, oppressing my heart and my body?

Maulana urges the Indian Muslims to invoke the Sufi mystics and spiritual luminaries who remembered Krishna on every Janmashtami to help mitigate the communal disharmony in the country. Their pluralistic messages in India should be rejuvenated, creating an atmosphere in which selfless service and unconditional love are one's only religion, he avered. See the following Urdu verses:

Irfan-E-Ishq Naam Hai Mere Maqam Ka

Hamil Hoon kis Ke Naghma-E-Nai Ke Payaam Ka

Gokul Ki Sarzameen Bhi Azeez-e-Jahan Bani

Kalma Padha Jo Unki Muhabbat Ke Naam Ka

Labrez-E-Noor Hai Dil-E-Hasrat Zahe-Naseeb

Ek Husn-e-Mushkfaam Ke Shauq-e-Tamaam Ka

The Divine Lovers Sees in Ram, Rasool!

Hai Ram Ke Wajood Pe Hindustan Ko Naz,

Ahl-e-Nazar Samajhte Hain Jinko Imam-E-Hind!

Translation: The land of India takes its pride on Rama's existence, the discerning eye sees in Ram, a prophet.

Allama Iqbal

Every nation was bestowed with a Prophet according to the holy Qur'an: *"And We certainly sent into every nation a messenger"* (Surah An-Nahl: 36). For Sufi Mystics, India, Bharat or Hindustan has been a sacred land of their Prophets too. Needless to state that India is thus the land to which Allah has sent most Messengers in all likelihood and strong probability. If an ancient philosophy of religious pluralism (Sarva Dharma Sama Bhava) and peaceful coexistence of various faith traditions has historically been recorded here, the reason is not difficult to see. The Message of all Seers and Sage—from Rishi Munis, Prophets, Mystics, to the Sufis—was One. Mahatma

Gandhi interpreted this concept as the one that embodies the equality of the destination of the different paths followed by different people. "The Truth is One but the Wise call it by many names", says the Maha Upanishad.

An over 5,000-year-old civilisation with various faith traditions, Mother India birthed Hinduism, Buddhism, Jainism and Sikhism and widely embraced Islam which converged in a spiritual synergy of Sufism. And it was only in India where the pluralistic Persianite strain of Islam emerged with the coming of Sufi saints from Central Asia. There were some sages and mystics among them who saw Rasool (prophet) in Rama and Krishna. Take a look at the following passage (Letter No. 14, Maqamat-e-Mazhari, Page No. 259) authored by Shah Ghulam Ali Dehlvi. This shows how our ancient indigenous Indic tradition was looked at through the prism of purely Sufi Islamic perspective. This book has been compiled in the light of the letters written by Mirzā Mazhar Jaan-e-Janan:

"India and the Hindu community from a theological viewpoint: In the Indian territories, Prophets and Messengers were sent by Allah Almighty. Their accounts are recorded in their books and several other signs and indicators tell us that the Hindu people had reached high culminations [in faith and spirituality]. The Divine mercy did not forget this vast land or its people and their state of affairs. Needless to say, before the Prophet Muhammad (PBUH), every nation was bestowed with a Prophet, and every community was entitled to follow their own Prophet rather than anyone else".

Mirzā Mazhar Jaan-e-Janan (1699–1780) was an authoritative Islamic saint-scholar of the Naqshbandi Sufi Order, which was established in India by Khwaja Baqi Billah (d. 1603)—Delhi's most prominent Naqshbandi master. He was instrumental behind the inclusivist legacy and pluralist theology of Shah Ghulam Ali Dehlvi—the 19th century Sufi master of the Naqshbandi Order in Delhi. For today's Indian Muslims, Mirzā Mazhar Jaan-e-Janan (Soul of the Souls) and Ghulam Ali Dehlvi offers much to reflect upon, as proponents of *Wahdat-e-Wahy* (unity in scriptures and divine revelations) between the Qur'an and the Vedas. Consider the crucial memoir as follows:

He [Jaan-e-Janan] was staying at Sirhind (a city in Punjab popularly known as Fatehgarh Sahib). I sought and obtained the permission to visit the master. My heart was instantaneously enticed and ensnared by the charismatic saint. He tied the game of his heart to the saddle straps of my spiritual course. I was particularly attracted to the teachings of his Exalted Presence (Jaan-e-Jana), that the Vedas were Holy Scriptures revealed by Allah, and that Shri Krishna and Shri Rama were Prophets; thus Jaan-e-Janan privileged the Hindus as the 'People of the Book'. (As quoted in "The Mirror of Beauty", By Shamsur Rahman Faruqi, 2014).

The Letter No. 14 in **Maqamat-e-Mazhari** examines the Vedic notion of Avatarvad, in accordance with the Islamic concept of Nubuwwat and Risalat (prophethood). Based on the Qur'anic verses such as "*There is a Messenger for every community*" (Surah al-R'ad: 07) and "*There was not a Nation without a warner*" (36:06), the letter premises that Allah has created no community in the world without a Prophet, and that belief in all Prophets, not just one, is one of the six articles of the Islamic faith. It then looks at the main characteristics of the Hindu belief of *Avatarvad* and Prophethood from an Islamic perspective.

This terrain of thought in Indian Muslim theology was further accentuated by Allama Muhammad Iqbal, the poet-philosopher popularly known as the Wise of Umma (Hakeem ul Ummat) in the Indian subcontinent. The Poet of the East (Shaer-e-Mashriq) took the temerity to proclaim the prophethood of Shri Rama and composed the following verses which speak volumes about his devoutness for Rama:

Labrez Hai Sharab-I-Haqiqat Se Jam-e-Hind!

Sab Falsafi Hain Khitta-i-Maghrib Ke Ram-e-Hind

Yeh Hindiyon Ke Fikr-i-Falak Ras Ka Hai Asar,

Rifat Men Asman Se Bhi Uncha Hai Bam-e-Hind

Rifat Men Asman Se Bhi Uncha Hai Bam-E-Hind

Is Des Men Huey Hain Hazaron Malak Sarisht,

Mashoor Jinke Dam Se Hai Duniya Men Nam-e-Hind

Hai Ram Ke Wajood Pe Hindostan Ko Naaz,

Ahle Nazar Samajhte Hain Usko Imam-E-Hind!

Ejaz Us Chiragh-E-Hidayat Ka Hai Yahi

Raushan Tar As Sahar Hai Zamane Men Sham-E-Hind!

Talwar Ka Dhani Tha, Shujat Men Fard Tha!

Pakeezgi Men Josh-E-Mohabbat Men Fard Tha!

Translation:

The cup of Hind overflows with the wine of truth.

Even philosophers of the West are its devotees.

The mysticism of her philosophers makes Hind's star soar above all constellations.

Thousands of angels have descended to proclaim Hind's name before the world.

And proud of his existence the discerning eye sees in Ram, a prophet.

The glow from this lamp of wisdom makes Hind's evening more radiant than the world's daybreak.

Valorous, brave, a master swordsman!

In purity, and in love, Rama was unmatched.

The above Urdu *Nazm* of Allama Iqbal is part of his poetic work, Bāng-e-Darā (The Call of the Marching Bell). It is seen as an unmatched and extraordinary tribute to the persona of Shri Rama.

However, while the Allama eulogises Shri Rama as Imam-e-Hind (Spiritual leader of India), in yet another poem, he cautions us against the waywardness of the priestly class Brahmins who misuse his name and are not true to his teachings and spiritual ideals and Dharmic legacy.

While it is an opportune time for Muslims to recall the Ummah's Wise Man, Allama Iqbal's six inspiring couplets on Shri Rama, it is also about time for Hindus of India to reflect on the actual meaning and essence of Ram-bhakti and discern between the veneration of Rama and its political expressions. While at Ayodhya, let's not forget the *vanavasa* – forest-dwelling and return of Shri Rama to Ayodhya after 14 years of exile. It offers us all a great learning to be evolved into a replica of the divine qualities; love, justice, forbearance, forgiveness and righteousness.

An Abode of Spiritual Symbiosis—
My Visit to Ayodhya

Reflections on the historicity and sanctity of the holy city of Ayodhya from a Sufi perspective!

As a madrasa student in Jamia Islamia, Raunahi Faizabad in 2005, I had an opportunity to visit the birthplace of Shri Rama in Ayodhya. This so happened that I was appearing for an examination called, maulvi/Munshi as part of Uttar Pradesh Board of Madarsa Education where I met a local Muslim leader and social activist from Ayodhya, Dr Ambar Siddiqui. He took me to the Ram Janmabhoomi, and revealed that in Indo-Islamic tradition, Ajodhya had assumed a paramount position. Prominent prophets and messengers of Allah such as Nabi Sheesh A.S (Prophet Sheth) were buried in this sacred city. Thus, the historicity and sanctity of Ajodhya stands out in my memory and spiritual consciousness since my Madrasa student life. According to numerous reports, the grave of Nabi Nooh A.S (Prophet Noah) locally known as *"26 Ghazi Mazar"*, which I visited, is also there.

The moment I entered the marked birthplace of Shri Rama, my early mystical experience at the age of 15 knew a new dimension. It was the first time I explored India as the land of Ambiya (Prophets) and *Auliya* (Saints), and Shri Rama as one of the earliest Indian Prophets who were a Divine Light to the people of this age-old civilization.

In Sufism, a Prophet is actually a Noori Bashar (a person of divine light) whereas in the Wahhabi view, every prophet is merely a Bashar (just like a common human being). Some Sufi saints of India went to the extent of believing Prophets as 'Avatars of Allah' (the descendants of the Divine Himself), and thus they understood the Islamic concept of Prophethood in terms of '*Avtarvad*. For instance—famous Sufi poet Sheikh Abdul Aleem Aasi Ghazipuri, a revered elder of Khanqah-e-Rashidiya, composed an Urdu couplet in praise of Prophet Muhammad (pbuh) as follows:

Wahi Jo Mustawwi-e-Arsh Hai Khuda Ho Kar

Utar Pada Hai Madine Mein Mustafa Ho Kar

(Translation: The One who ascends the Throne/Arsh as Allah has ascended in Madina as Mustafa/Muhammad PBUH)

The above esoteric Sufi couplet and its interpretation, of course, is a matter of contention with orthodox Muslims, but it is close to what Hindus would easily absorb. In fact, for Hindus who collectively believe in the divinity of all Avatars, this should not be contentious at all.

Therefore, I find that it is incumbent upon Muslims in today's India to revisit the spiritual historicity and sanctity of Ayodhya. They must look at Ayodhya as an abode of spiritual symbiosis and not allow the episode of Babri Masjid dominate their thoughts and colour their understanding.

Ayodhya has been the land of both Rishi-Munis as well as Ambiya and Rusul (Prophets and Messengers of Allah) in the ancient ages. Needless to state that every nation was bestowed with a Prophet according to the Qur'an: *"And We certainly sent into every nation a messenger"*.

In fact, Ayodhya has been considered the land of Ambiya and Awiliya Allah as recorded in Abul Fazl's **Ain-i-Akbari**. It has been looked up to with great veneration in the undivided India by not just Hindus but also Muslims. According to **Aaain-e-Akbari**, Ayodhya has assumed great significance in Muslim history and religious consciousness. Apart from scores of mosques (around 100 big mosques and 54 small ones), the historic city houses 22 Sufi shrines, several dargahs and Mazars, 15 Imam Baadas as well as 100 Qabristans (Muslim cemeteries).

In the Mughal period, the Muslim population in Ayodhya was around 67% thus making the city a Muslim-majority part of the country. It is quite interesting to note that even today, a great many Mohallas and Qasbas in Ayodhya are named after Prophets and Sufi Saints. For instance, "Nabi Nooh Mohalla", "Nabi Sheesh Mohalla", "Mohalla Shah Qalandar", "Shamsuddin Mohalla", "Syed Ibrahim Nagri", "Syed Shah Mohalla" are some of the most noteworthy Mohallas in the densely populated city of Ayodhya.

The history of Indian Sufi saints shows us that Ayodhya also has been the birthplace of several prominent pupils of the chief Chishti Saint of Delhi, Hazrat Khwaja Nizamuddin Auliya (R.A). Famous among them was Hazrat Khwaja Naseeruddin Chiragh Dehlvi, popularly known as "Chiragh-e-Dilli". All of these Chishti saints showed great reverence for the city of Ayodhya, not because it had the Babri Masjid in it, but rather because it has been an abode of Ambiya and Auliya, just as it was greatly venerated among the Rishi-Munis and Hindu mystics. Some of the prominent Sufi shrines located in Ayodhya are as under:

Dargah Hazrat Nooh A.S.

Dargah Hazrat Sheesh A.S.

Syed Shah Muqaddas Dargah

Teen Darvesh Ki Dargah

Makhdoom Shah Dargah

Shah Jamal Dargah

Shah Qalandar Dargah

Jamaluddin Qazi Dargah

Qazi Muhiyuddin Kashani Dargah

Zainuddin Ali Dargah

Kamaluddin Awadhi Dargah

Dargah Syed Muhammad Ibrahim

Shaheed Martaba Dargah

Shamsuddin Faryad Dargah

Fathullah Shah Dargah

Syed Alauddin Qarsani Dargah

Sultan Moosa Dargah

Alauddin Ali Dargah

Shaikh Fathullah Awadhi Dargah

Jamaluddin Ghazi Dargah

Aastana Hazrat Sheikh ul Aalam Makhdoom

Dargah Hazrat Sayyed Makhdoom Shah Bheeka Makki

Astana Shaikh Sayyah Baba

Hazrat Faizullah Shah Badi Dargah

Mazar Hazrat Aashiq Shah Madni Warsi

Dargah Saheed E Millat

Ayodhya has historically been famous for the festivals and occasions where Muslims and Hindus have jointly gathered in great joy and festivity. Muhammad Faiz Bakhsh, author of Tareekh-e-Farah Bakhsh notes that Hindus had a big mela (gathering) in which thousands of Muslims used to participate. In his *Masnawi*, Mir Hasan Dehlvi has also made a special mention of those Hindu occasions in Awadh and Ayodhya where Muslims took part in great numbers.

In the City of the Most Beloved Madina Munawara

The beautiful story of how the Prophet's city was built with love and my recent visit to his tomb in Madina—Roza-e-Rasool…..

Recently, this writer got blessed by a non-obligatory spiritual pilgrimage to Makkah called *'Umrah'*, a shorter version of the annual obligatory Hajj. On this sacred occasion, Hajj and Umrah pilgrims pay a special visit to the holy city of Masjid an-Nabawi in Madina Munawwara-- which is the holiest city after Makka al-Mukarram in Islam. For, it is the abode of the holy Prophet Muhammad (pbuh), and he is reported to have said in a hadith reported in Sunan al-Daraqutni:

"من زار قبري وجبت له شفاعتي"

(Whoever visits my grave, she/he will be surely granted my greatest intercession, *shafa'at*)

This hadith has been authenticated and strengthened by Hafidh Taqi al-Din al-Subki, highly venerated among the Sufi Orders as a great Qur'an exegete, Asha'ri scholar and *Shafi'i* jurist. Although the followers of Ibn Taymiyah and Ibn Abdul Wahhab i.e. the Salafis and Hanbalis particularly in Saudi Arabia dismiss this Prophetic Tradition, Indian Muslims at large adhere to it with great love and devotion for the holy Prophet (pbuh). Thus, highly venerated by Indian Muslims, Madina Munawara earns greater attention especially during the sacred days of Hajj and Umrah pilgrimages.

Masjid Nabawi (Prophetic Mosque), Madinah Munawwara

In general, the holy city of Madina Munawara is revered by all Muslims across the world because one of the two holiest sites of Islam, the Prophet's mosque or Masjid-e-Nabawi is located in it. After the *Kaaba* which is the first place of worship in the Abrahamic faith traditions built by Hazrat Ibrahim A.S and located in Masjid al-Haram, Masjid al-Nabawi is the second holiest site in Islam. This is the main significance of Madina among Muslims which is further sanctified by another sacred site situated in the same holy city—*Masjid-e-Quba*—the first mosque of Islam in *Madina Munawwara*

Significantly for Sufi Muslims around the world and especially in India, the first Sufi seminary of Islam known as "*Dar us-Suffa*", is also located within *Masjid al-Nabawi.*

There was a special group of the mystically inclined companions (*Sahaba)* of the holy Prophet (PBUH) called *Ashab us-Suffa*. They used to engage in mystical brainstorming in a systematic way and regularly attended the formal spiritual learning in *Dar us-Suffa* provided by the Prophet (pbuh).

Most significantly, the story of the construction of Masjid-e-Nabawi should move the Muslims of today. As the Prophet (Pbuh) and his companions were migrants from Makkah, they were called *"al-Muhajirin"*. And the local inhabitants of Madinah who welcomed the *Muhajirin* and greatly helped them were known as Al-Ansar (the helpers). The Ansar belonged to the two main tribes of Madinah, the Banu Khazraj and the Banu Aus, who had an age-old rivalry. But the Holy Prophet (PBUH) established brotherhood (*Muwakhat*) and mutual sympathy (*Mouwasat*) between the two adversary tribes. These were the prophetic ideals which ushered in an era of spiritual bond between the two different tribes in Madinah- both helping each other, in every way possible.

The Ansar of Madinah assisted the Muhajirin by hosting them in their homes and providing for their financial and material necessities. Remarkably, both the Ansar and Muhajirin took active part in the construction of Al-Masjid an-Nabawi in particular and the entire city of Madina. This bond of brotherhood among the two different tribes was inspired by the holy Prophet's spiritual training and instructions. He exhorted them both: "Act together in your daily efforts and then share the fruits of your labour among yourselves."

While the Ansar and Muhajirin were labouring and toiling hard in the construction of Masjid-e-Nabawi, the holy Prophet (pbuh) invoked Allah: *"O Allah! Help the Ansar and the Muhajirin in strengthening a strong relationship between them."*

The Prophet built the brotherly ties not only between the Ansar and Muhajirin but also among the different religious tribes of Madina who were earlier at loggerheads. Consequently, the *Ansar* and *Muhajirin* were strengthened by a third group – the Jews of Madinah. The holy Prophet (pbuh) thus built a cohesive society in Madina where Muslims and Jews peacefully coexisted and shared their joys and grief. They professed and practised two different faiths and yet there was such an amicable relationship between Muslims and Jews that if anyone harmed a Jew, the first aid came from the Muslims of Madina – both *Ansar* and *Muhajirin*. This is how a harmonious, affectionate and cohesive society was built in the city of the holy Prophet – Madinah.

Today, Muslims from across the world, especially from our country, India visit and venerate the sacred shrine of the holy Prophet (pbuh) to seek his blessings and find spiritual solace.

The holy Prophet was born in Makka but he chose to migrate to Madina after he faced religious persecution at the hands of the Makkan pagans. While he was persecuted in Makka, people of Madina welcomed the Prophet (pbuh) with open arms and great warmth. Therefore, *Madina Munawara* has great significance and sanctity in the spiritual Islamic traditions, especially in Sufism. After the completion of the *Manasik-e-Hajj* (rituals of the Haj), it is highly recommended by the Sufi saints to perform *Ziyarat* of *Rauza e Rasool* (visitation of the Prophet's holy shrine), which is one of the most magnificent Islamic heritage in Madina.

Besides the sacred shrine of the holy Prophet and the mosque of the Prophet (*Masjid-e-Nabawi*), *Jannat ul-Baqi* – the graveyard of the Prophet's noble family, Ahl-e-Bayt and many companions and early spiritual masters of Islam – has also a great place in Sufism.

The Martyrs of Divine Love

Imam Hussain and the "Hussaini Brahmins"

Hind Mein Kaash Hussain Ibn-e-Ali Aaa Jaate

Choomte Unke Qadam Palke Bichate Hindu

Jang Karne Yahan Shabbir Se Aata Jo Yazeed

Usko Rawan Ki Tarah Dhool Chataate Hindu

Translation: Had Imam Hussain come to India, he would have been greatly venerated and revered by the Hindus. If Yazid were here to wage a war against the Imam, Hindus would have defeated him the way they humiliated the Ravana)

While commemorating Muharram and recalling Imam Hussain's martyrdom, we Muslims often forget those who stood by Hussain in his harshest times. Those who exerted concerted efforts to fight for truth and justice, though they did not belong to Islam, the religion of Imam.

One of the most notable, but regrettably forgotten supporters of Imam Hussain was an Indian community historically traced as "Hussaini brahmins". A little-known group and small in numbers, the Hussaini brahmins also known as Dutt community and Mohiyals, mainly found in Punjab, are traced back to the event of Karbala which occurred in 680 AD. These Punjabi Brahmins are those whose ancestors fought for Imam Hussain in Karbala. The story goes on:

Fast as wind, carving their way through the sand, dunes at lightning speed, a caravan of few Indian sons in a noble pursuit, was making its way towards Karbala to register their names in the pages of history.

'Hal Min Nasirin Yansurna': Is there anyone who can help me?

When Prophet Muhammad's Grandson Imam Husain posed this question to humanity, History witnessed that while Kalma-reciting Muslims were out there to slit his throat, far from his battlefield in Karbala, some brave Indians left their homes to support Imam Husain striving for the truth and righteousness. These were those brave Indians who travelled to Karbala to write a golden page in the history of age-old Hindu-Muslim Unity.

The ongoing Islamic month of Muharram marks a turning point in our Indian history too. On the auspicious 10th of Muharram, Imam Hussain attained martyrdom and rescued humanity from the clutches of evil. He refused to surrender to the Tyrant Yazid, who created a dictatorial dynasty deviating from the consensual democracy (Shur'a) in Islam. Therefore, the noble sacrifice of Imam Hussain is looked up as the revival of the true Islamic principles of democracy, justice, fairness and mutual consensus in the matters of governance.

The Tyrant Yazid, high on his power, was adamant on bringing shame to humanity. But he knew as long as Imam Husain was alive, he wouldn't succeed in his nefarious ends. It was because of this fear that Yazid cornered Imam Husain and his family at Karbala and forced him to bow down to his tyranny. A living example of valiance and indefatigable determination, Imam Husain proposed that either he would live in Madina on his conditions, or he would migrate to India (Hindustan).

None of these peaceful proposals was accepted by the Tyrant Yazid. Rather, the innocent Imam and all his clan and noble family were cornered near the River of Euphrates, Darya-e-Furat in Iraq. They were tortured and persecuted so much so that even water was denied to their little children, toddlers and their mothers. Even 6-month-old Ali Asghar, the youngest son of Imam, was killed by the Tyrants in an extreme hunger and thirst for water. And all these atrocities were executed on a written order from Yazid.

As they say, people remember the dearest ones and the real well-wishers in their tough times.

While Imam Husain wrote a letter seeking help from his childhood friend Habib in Arabia, his elder son Ali Akbar wrote a similar letter and sent it far away from Karbala…very far to India….. to a Hindustani Sapoot and King of India, Raja Samudargupt who happened to be a cousin-brother of Ali-ibn-e Husain.

Strange as it may sound, History is witness to this unlikely relationship. Over 1400 years ago, the king of Iran, a Parsi by faith, had two daughters—Maher Bano and Shaher Bano. Maher Bano was married to King Chandragupt and was renamed Chandralekha. A few years later, Canderlekha's younger sister, Shaher Bano, was married to Imam Husain

A.S. Chandralekha and Chandergupt's son Samudargupt was the King of India when he got the letter from his cousin Ali ibn-E-Husain.

King Samudargupt swiftly arranged for a group of brave Indian soldiers and ordered them to depart towards Karbala. The army commander was Rehab Dutt, a Mohiyal Brahmin. Unfortunately, by the time Rehab Dutt and his brave-heart soldiers reached Karbala, Imam Husain was killed. This news disheartened the entire Indian troupe. They decided to run their swords on their own necks. "When the one we came to help is no more, what should we do with these swords?' they asked. Just then, an Arab admirer of Imam Husain persuaded them to take the swords off their necks and join the force of Janab-e-Mukhtar. Thus, these Indian soldiers fought a memorable battle, exhibiting the best of Hindustani swords in Karbala to avenge the death of Imam Husain A.S.

Even today, the place of Karbala where these brave Brahmins resided is called '*ad-Diyar-al-Hindiyya*'. Some of these Brahmins were martyred at Karbala, some stayed back, while few returned to Mother India. History remembers these Brave Brahmins by the name of 'Husaini Brahmins'. Today, we must salute this lesser known but truly great saga of Hindu-Muslim Unity.

These Rajput Mohiyals or the Dutt family from India fulfilled the sacred vision of the holy Prophet when he said: I feel the fragrance coming from India. These "Hussaini brahmins" also strengthen the beautiful blend of our Indo-Islamic tradition. In the words of a Hindustani poet:

Wah Dutt Sultan,

Hindu ka Dharm, Musalman ka Iman,

Adha Hindu, Adha Musalman!

(Bravo! O Dutt, the king who follows the Hindu religion as well as the Muslim faith, and is a half Hindu and a half Musalman)

Famous Indian film actor Sunil Dutt also belonged to Rahab Dutt's family, and hence was a 'Hussaini brahmin'. He used to commemorate the martyrdom of Imam Hussain by himself in the footsteps of his ancestors on the occasion of the holy month of Muharram. In this context, the Muharram processions and commemorations organized by Husaini Brahmins in memory of Imam Hussain is the best example of the inclusiveness of Indo-Islamic tradition. Most notably, the members of the Dutt family did not leave their religion and while being Hindus, they told humanity that Hussainiyyat is an integral part of their faith. This is indeed a rare and unique albeit lesser known historically recorded story of divine love. Even today the sons and daughters of those courageous divine lovers—Hussaini Brahmins— live among us without us even knowing them. For instance— the famed actor and nationalist Indian politician Sunil Dutt and his son and film actor Sanjay Dutt are often mentioned. Besides these two famous Indian celebrities, Hindu-Urdu writers such as Sabir Dutt and Nand Kishore Vikram are also some of the notable Hussaini brahmins.

An Untold Story of Divine Love

"Sar-ba-Kaf"—when *Sufi Mystic & Martyr* Sarmad Shaheed began to dance with his head on the steps of the Jama Masjid in his divine love!

Jama Masjid, Delhi

Inspired by this incredible incident, this writer feels impelled to tell the story of Jama Masjid, the magnificent mosque which stands out in the annals of history as an emblem of Indo-Islamic art and architecture and its beautiful aesthetics. Built by the Mughal Emperor Shahjahan in 1656 and designed by Ustad Ahmad Lahori, the mosque beautifully reflects the Indo-Islamic style of architecture imbued with Arabic, Persian and indigenous architectural influences. The structure oriented towards the holiest city of Islam, Makkah was made from red sandstone with white marble inlay. Incredibly, it sits on an elevated stone platform that is accessible by stairs from the eastern, northern, and southern entrances. Over 5000 artisans under the supervision of Wazir Saadullah Khan took the uphill task of accomplishing the construction of Jama Masjid with the amazing architectural features adorning it and making it worthy of great visitations from around the world. But the real story of Jama Masjid is little known and untold.

Authentic legends tell us that during the Mughal Period, when Emperor Shahjahan was entirely engaged in the construction of royal palaces and magnificent buildings in the then Shahjahanabad [now Old Delhi], he also thought of constructing a great towering mosque in Delhi. For years, this could not be decided as to what shape the mosque should take. However, one night the king saw a beautiful mosque in his dream which he took as a helping hint from the Almighty Divine. But by the time he woke up, the image of his dream faded out from his mind.

Shahjahan was so sad. In quest of his confusion, he called for an immediate meeting in his court and narrated his dream. They had a long discussion on this dream but they could not arrive at a conclusion. Ultimately, Shahjahan ordered his Diwan Sa'adullah Khan to announce an ordinance in public, stating that, "whoever shall submit a Map or Design of His dream mosque would be highly rewarded from the treasury of the King".

After this announcement, a lot of designs and maps were presented to the King but none of them was approved of. At last, Fazil Khan, a cook who was also a close disciple of Hazrat Hare Bhare Shah Khwaja Sayyed Abul Qasim Sabzwari (R.A.) presented his design. Drawn by Fazil Khan, this design was found to be closest to the image of King's dream mosque and as per the royal announcement, Fazil Khan was chosen for the promised Award.

But Fazil Khan did not accept the award. He rather requested that his award be first handed over to his Murshid, the honourable Sufi Master of Delhi in his times, Hazrat Khwaja Sayyed Abul Qasim Sabzwari popularly known as Hare Bhare Shah. Although Shahjahan had heard his name, the value and virtue of Hare Bhare Shah was introduced only that day. He immediately ordered for preparation of his visit to Hare Bhare Shah. Emperor Shahjahan and Fazil Khan both went together to meet the Sufi Sheikh and they were received with great warmth and affection. Hare Bhare Shah accepted the award and then bestowed that upon Fazil Khan, and offered lots of dua'a for the king.

Notably, Hazrat Bhare Shah was a nature-lover Sufi saint of Delhi. He used to live in the valley of Mount Hajlah where both Shahjahan's Dream Mosque as well as his sacred shrine were built. The shrine of Hare Bhare right in the heart of Old Delhi, just below the steps of the Jama Masjid, is truly unique with a neem tree growing above it. Besides the courtyard of Hazrat Hare Bhare Shah is the grave of the famous 'dancing dervish' of Delhi, Sarmad Kashani more popular as Sarmad Shaheed, originally a Jewish mystic and a Persian-speaking Armenian poet who travelled as a spiritual pilgrim and turned into an Indian Sufi and made the Indian subcontinent his permanent home during the 17th century. While his spiritual mentor or Murshid's tomb is green in colour to donate immortality, Sarmad Shaheed's grave is red to mark his martyrdom.

Maulana Azad who was a great admirer of Sufi Sarmad Shaheed and his concept of "Divine Love" (Ishq-e-Haqiqi), was reportedly a frequent visitor to his shrine. In the words of Sarover Zaidi, a social anthropologist, Sarmad's shrine is "not just a built structure but also a performance—of his life and death, his ideas, his poetry as also his love, rebellion and critique of the social order. It provides space to that which cannot be ordered, that which falls off the confines of orthodox religion, worship and societal norms; it provides solace to ideas of love and rebellion, annotated so fantastically in the red that is at once familiar and shocking".

Today, the Jama Masjid is famed as the largest mosque of Delhi with no parallel to it in the entire country. It served as the imperial mosque of the Mughal emperors until the demise of the empire in 1857. In fact, the first freedom movement of India--the 1857 revolt against the British was supported by a Fatwa from the same Jama Masjid. Right from Allama Fazle Haque Khairabadi to Maulana Abul Kalam Azad, Ulama who stood for the Indian freedom movement spoke from Jama Masjid's Mimbar (pulpit) to the Muslims of India. In 1947, during a Friday prayer of 23rd October, Maulana Aazad delivered a sermon from its pulpit or Mimbar when the Partition of India was underway, causing massive damage and population movements in Delhi. Azad implored the Muslims of Delhi to remain in

India, and attempted to reassure them that India was still their homeland. He spoke highly of his belongingness to Islam as his religion and India as his nation:

"I am a Muslim and profoundly conscious of the fact that I have inherited Islam's glorious traditions of the last 14 hundred years. I am not prepared to lose even a small part of that legacy...I am equally proud of the fact that I am an Indian, an essential part of the invisible unity of Indian nationhood, a vital factor in its total make-up without which its noble edifice will remain incomplete.

The tomb of Maulana Abul Kalam Azad is also located adjacent to the mosque. Today, Jama Masjid remains in active use during Ramadan, Eid-ul-Fitr, Eid-ul-Adha, Eid Milad-un-Nabi, and is one of Delhi's most iconic sites, closely identified with the ethos of 'Purani Dilli' i.e. Old Delhi or Delhi 6. Hazrat Hare Bhare Sahib lived in Delhi during the Period of Jahangir, Shah Jahan and Aurangzeb and he is believed to have inspired and initiated Sarmad Shaheed who was originally an Armenian Jew. The most compelling imagination at this historic mosque is the imagery of Sarmad walking up the stairs of Jama Masjid with his head in his hand. Great modernist Muslim artist of recent times, Syed Sadequain Ahmed Naqvi drew out a whole series titled *Sar-ba-Kaf* inspired by this imagery. "Lingering possibly at each corner of such a vivid and repeated imagery is the idea of a dialogue with the self. Each story of chopped heads is as much about the social as it is about ourselves," writes Sarover Zaidi.

Tellingly, Sarmad began to dance on the steps of the Jama Masjid after his head was cut off on the orders of Emperor Aurangzeb (on the fanatic fatwa of the clergymen declaring him a 'heretic'). It was only due to Hare Bhare Shah that he stopped doing that. For, he warned the dead body of Sarmad that if it didn't stop, it would completely destroy Delhi.

Significantly, Hazrat Hare Bhare Shah Khwaja Abul Qasim Sabzwari came from Sabzwar in Iran. His teachings were peaceful and pluralistic as he preached the oneness of God and brotherhood of Mankind. And he followed and practised the beautiful traditions of the holy Prophet (pbuh). It is believed that the holy Prophet appeared in a dream of the Sufi saint and praised the mosque adoring its magnificent architecture. Therefore, an area of the mosque where the Prophet is believed to have appeared in the vision, has been barricaded in the ablution tank (Hauz) to show respect and veneration to the holy Prophet. Also, a stone with the footprint of the holy Prophet along with many other Relics are also preserved in the heart of Jama Masjid as part of what is called Dargah Asaar Sharif. As Delhi is the heart of India, Jama Masjid is the heart of Delhi, and the heart of Jama Masjid is *Aasar Sharif*--the relics of the holy Prophet (peace be upon him)!

Baba Farid—Punjabi-Sufi Saint and his Pursuit of Peace in Palestine

India's peace-making efforts in Jerusalem could be traced back to over 800 years ago when the prominent Indian Sufi saint of the Chishti order, Hazrat Baba Farid Ganj Shakar from Ajodhan. Since then, Sufi mystics from across the world have come to Jerusalem with their divine music, whirling and ecstasy, and have been engaged in a spiritual battle for peace in Palestine. In the old holy city of Jerusalem, there is still a place called Al-Zawiyya Al-Hindiyya—Indian hospice (also known as Al-Hindi Sarai or Indian lodge), where Baba Farid lived and meditated in the early 13th century. Traditionally, Indian pilgrims have gathered at Baba Farid's lodge, bringing with them instruments and melodies from the famous Indian province of Punjab. Sufis have been singing verses written by Baba Farid and poems and hymns from Guru Granth Sahib, the central scripture in Sikhism.

We don't exactly know how long Baba Farid stayed in the holy city of Jerusalem. However, long after he had returned to the Punjab, where he eventually became head of the Chishti Sufi order, Indian Muslims passing through Jerusalem on their way to Mecca started to pray where he had prayed. Thus, over a period of time, a holy shrine or lodge called, the Indian Hospice, was formed in the memory of Baba Farid.

Known in Arabic as al-Zawiyya al-Hindiyya or "Zawiyat al-Hunud", this Indian Sufi hospice or Khanqah in Jerusalem greatly marks the great historic contributions that the Indian mystics have rendered as peacemakers. As the legend has it, Baba Farid came to the old city of Jerusalem around the year 1200, and meditated in a stone lodge for 40 days. Ever since, Indian Muslim pilgrims on their way to or from Mecca have been attracted to the site and eventually it became the Indian Hospice. The Zawiyah has been extensively documented.

Baba Farid arrived in Jerusalem at a time when the holy city had just returned to Muslim hands after almost a century of Christian rule. The Crusaders, ensconced along the Mediterranean coast, had not gone away, and Salahuddin Ayyubi understood that if Muslims were to keep Jerusalem, they would need to match the Crusaders not only on the battlefield but in their spiritual veneration of the city as well. It was the Indian Sufi Baba Farid who realised and translated it into reality.

Since then, Sufi mystics have been drawn to Jerusalem from across the world. Some Sufis who came to Jerusalem were barefoot drifters. They wandered from town to town in search of solace and tranquillity. They mostly wore rough woollen robes and slept in the desert. They wept in the pain of people and sang for the love of God. Thus, the Sufis in

Jerusalem, with their music, whirling and ecstasy, have been engaged in a spiritual battle for peace in Palestine.

When Sultan Salahuddin Ayyubi re-consecrated Jerusalem and had the rock beneath the golden dome, he welcomed Sufi saints with open arms and encouraged popular devotion to the holy city's cultural and spiritual heritage, shrines and sanctuaries. In this beautiful historical ambience, Indian pilgrims gathered at Baba Farid's lodge, bringing with them instruments and melodies from the famous Indian province of Punjab. Since then in Jerusalem, these Sufi seekers have been singing verses written by Baba Farid and his disciple, Guru Nanak Dev. This beautiful peace poetry in Palestine binds together the Sufi and Sikh traditions of India in Jerusalem. Dozens of Baba Farid's poems and hymns are found in the Guru Granth Sahib, the central scripture in Sikhism which is a compilation of mystical verses.

The medieval traveller Evliya Chelebi has identified Al Zawiya Al Hindiyya—the Indian Hospice—as one of the largest Zawiyahs in the city in 1671. Over the next 300 or 400 years, Sufi travellers from across the world have joined the Indians in Jerusalem in the construction of therapeutic Sufi centres, hospitals, schools and lodges that have housed mystics from Morocco and the Crimea, Anatolia and Uzbekistan.

Hasrat Mohani and his Syncretic Divine Love

India's prominent Sufi mystic, Urdu and Persian poet and Muslim freedom-fighter was an embodiment of communal harmony with his syncretic concept of divine love!

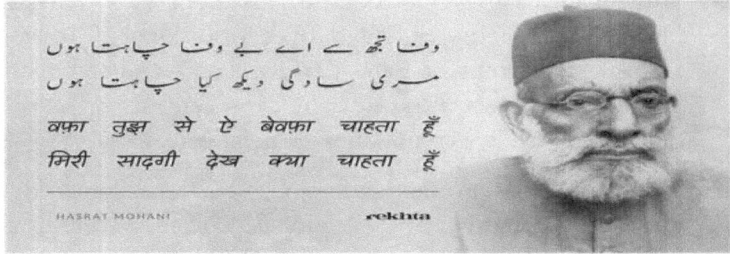

The well-known Urdu poet and freedom fighter, Maulana Hasrat Mohani was one of the Indian mystics who had celebrated divine love and syncretic devotion. He was in his own words, a Sufi *mo'min* (Sufi believer) and *ishtiraki* Muslim (secular Muslim), *Aashiq-e-Rasool* (lover of the Prophet) and a Krishn bhakt (Krishna devotee) at the same time.

It was Hasrat Mohani, who coined the revolutionary slogan 'Inquilab Zindabad!' with an aim to ignite the passion for freedom of India. His revolutionary idea of *Inqilab* was intertwined with his beautiful concept of *darweshi* (mysticism) which he showed as the ultimate path for the freedom of India as well as the liberation of Indian people's souls. This is precisely what he called for in many of his mesmerizing Urdu couplets like this:

Darweshi-o-inqilab maslak hai mera

Sufi momin hun, ishtiraki muslim

(Translation: Mysticism and Revolution are my creeds,

For I am a Sufi believer, as well as a Secular Muslim)

As a revolutionary ideologue of the 1947 freedom movement, Hasrat Mohani envisaged bringing together the two different religious communities—Hindus and Muslims—through his beautiful mystical concept of love for the 'Indian Prophets' which, in his view, included Shri Krishna. He called him 'Hazrat Krishn' and venerated him as a Prophet, and a noble, righteous, beloved messenger of God. He also offered theological bases, as laid out by several Indian Sufis like Hazrat Mazhar Jan-e-Janan, to prove that Krishna is a source of unity and accord between Hindus and Muslims in India. Mohani exhorted Indian Muslims not to forget the earlier prophets who had been sent down to various territories, according to the Qur'an. Thus, Mohani's poetry is full of love and devotion for 'Hazrat Krishn' in which he is revered as an embodiment of divine compassion, tenderness and mercy. Here is one such instance of Mohani's Urdu couplets in love for Krishna:

"To-se lagai Kanhaa preet

Kahu or kisurati ab aai kaahe

Hasrat Tan man dhan sab waar-ke

Mathura nagar ramaai chali dhooni"

(My heart has fallen in love with Kanhaiya. Why would anyone else think of it now? Hasrat, give up all that is yours for him. Then go to Mathura and become a jogi).

He also composed these couplets in praise for Krishna:

Irfan-e-ishq hai mere ka maqam

Hamil hoonkis ke payaam ka naghma-e-nai ke

Labrez-e-noor hai dil-e-Hasrat, and zahe-naseeb

Ikhusn-i-mushkfaam ke ka shauq-i-tamaam

(I stand where the perfect knowledge of love is found. Who is the flute whose melody fills me? What a good fortune, Hasrat, that your heart brims with a glowing love for the beauty of musk!)

The Maulana also issues a "fatwa" to justify his love for Krishan, considering the religious fanatics who may criticise his devotion to Krishna:

"Puna hoe na kipreet ka paap Shyam

Kou kaahe pashchatap karat hai

Neha ki aag maatan-pupa

Jalat rahi chup-chaap kab lag"

(Loving Shyam is not a sin, nor a virtue. So why do people repent? How long do I have to burn silently in the fire of love, oppressing my heart and my body?)

Today India's freedom fighters and mystic poets such as Maulana Hasrat Mohani must be remembered at a time when communal harmony is eroding in the country. His pluralistic messages in India should be revitalized, with the view to creating an environment in which love is the only religion.

Sufi Music—Listen to language of Divine Love!

Sufi music or sima'a is a universal language of love and harmony. At Hazrat Nizamuddin Auliya's Dargah in New Delhi, when the annual ceremony of Urs is held, a variety of cultural activities, including qawwali (popular Sufi music), *sima'a* (ceremony of whirling and listening to the Sufi recitals) and *zikr* (remembrance of God) are performed by the Sufi lovers and devotees amid a cyclone of rapture.

Across the world, Sufi lovers engage in sima a listening to different kinds of musical melodies coming from the heart. But the sole purpose is not merely playing a particular trend of Sufi music or promoting it, but rather connecting people's hearts to one another and thus attaining the divine pleasure with unity in multiplicity.

When our hearts connect with each other so closely, we attain Qalb-e-Hafiz (a heart that remembers) and thus we understand each other properly and amicably and, subsequently, acquire the hidden truths of the visible universe. Just as the popular Turkish folk or Sufi music—Mevlevi Sima'a—was conceived and evolved by Maulana Jalauddin Rumi, India's traditional Chishti Sima'a was popularised by Ameer Khusrau Dehlvi, the closest disciple of Hazrat Nizamuddin Aulia. An Indian poet at heart, Khusrau was actually the "father of Qawwali" as well as a scholar, philosopher, linguist and an influential Sufi saint himself. Writing his poetry mostly in Persian and Brij Bhasha (a language similar to Hindi), he used to weave his Hindavi songs and dohas into the oral transmissions and teachings of his Murshid (spiritual master), which were later collected in the famous Sufi document 'Fawa'id-ul-Fu'ad' (discourses benefiting the heart). Today, the audience at the Dargah Hazrat Nizamuddin Aulia soaks in the experience and understanding of the saint's words in his beautiful songs and dohas.

The Chishti sima'a is especially performed during the Urs occasions, out of an overflow of spiritual inclinations, with an adherence to certain Islamic guidelines. An integral and vital part of the Sima'a ceremony is the recital of Na'at (poetry in praise of the beloved Prophet) which is mostly composed in Urdu and Persian. Those listening to Na'at are exhorted to lend an ear and comprehend its profound meanings. Thus, they fall deep into spiritual ecstasy moving arbitrarily to the verses and couplets being sung by the naat khawans (reciters). Sufi music or sima'a is a universal language of love and harmony. But its popularity in India is attributed to Ameer Khusrau.

One does not find words to express the deeper spiritual emotions and mystical experiences that emanate from Khusrav's kalam (poetry). However, the most popular musical genres in his Chishti tradition are qawwalis and folk Sufi songs. Remarkably, while Khsrau's Hindawi dohas and riddles have reached us through oral traditions more than in written documents, they have enlightened the Indian masses, regardless of religion and creed, for more than seven centuries. Khusrau's all-time favourite kalam (couplets) which he composed for his beloved murshid, Hazrat Nizamuddin Aulia, is: "main to piya se naina mila ayi re" as well as "chhap tilak sab chini re mose naina milaike". Khusrau says in his ecstasy: "I play the game of love with my beloved, if I win, he is mine, and if I lose I am with him!"

India, the the Land of Mastkalandars–the Divine Lovers

August 15 was the day when we Indians began to breathe the air of freedom. This freedom, of course, brought decent life and basic human rights back to us. However, we tend to forget the remarkable contributions of many who built our nation, particularly those who developed a composite Indian culture with their mystically-inclined role. Our mystics had a fairly large share in creating a composite culture of our country.

India has been the land of mystics and Sufi saints. Sufism is anchored in humanism, universal brotherhood, peace and pluralism, compassion, goodwill and tolerance. It's in perfect harmony with the composite Indian culture. Sufi teachings are based on pluralistic traditions that are in sync with the notion of unity in diversity. Sufi saints preached moderate, progressive, multicultural and pluralistic Islamic tradition, which was the sole reason behind its popularity in the land of Vedic culture.

In contemporary India the impact of Sufism can be seen through the prism of arts and culture. The multifaceted Sufi tra-dition reflects an essentially pluralistic and composite culture that connects people of this country beyond many barriers. The most redeeming features of Sufism's appeal in India, as anywhere else, are its inherent openness, wide embrace, tolerance and its accommodating nature. No wonder then, a great many Indian Sufis, like Khwaja Gharib Nawaz Moinuddin Chishti of Ajmer, Baba Fariduddin of Pakpattan and Delhi's Qutbuddin Bakhtiyar Kaki, Hazrat

Nizamuddin Aulia and Chiragh Dilli left an everlasting and magnetic impact.

However, one regrets that the true spirit of Sufi culture and tradition in the country is now beginning to wane. It has been reduced to only occasional shrine visits, spiritual consultation or observance of particular routine rituals and festivals. Today's fakirs and pirs seem to have done away with their effort to keep alive the Sufism-inspired mystical culture of pluralism and moderation. Though they still engage in their occupations in the mazars that outnumber even mosques and madrasas in some areas, they seem to have lost their impact. Now their role is reduced to being peer-o-murshid (spiritual guru) to those who seek consultation in relation to their mundane worldly affairs.

Needless to say, Sufis and all mystically-inclined traditions of India have to reclaim and strengthen the spiritual foundations on which they are based. We should engage in creating a global spiritual fraternity through tawheed (oneness of God), *wahdatul wujud* (unity of existence), *ilmul yaqeen* (knowledge with certitude), *zikr* (incantation), *muraqaba* (meditation), *taqwa* (God-consciousness), *tawba* (repentance on sins), *ikhlas* (sincerity), *tawakkul* (contentment), *sidq* (truthfulness), *amanah* (trustworthiness), *istiqamah* (uprightness) and *shukr* (thankfulness).

India in view of Amir Khusrau

Khusrau's poetry and musical innovation continue to be part of the soul of Hindustani music.

An epitome of religious syncretism and Hindu-Muslim harmony, social cohesion and communal integration, Amir Khusrau, closest disciple of Hazrat Nizamuddin Aulia, is known as one of the founders of the Hindustani language — Hindi or Hindavi. Khusrau's teachings in the form of his Persian and Awadhi poetry stressed the pluralistic Indo-Islamic tradition. Born in 653, Khusrau was a spiritually inclined poet right from his childhood. But his avid inner devotion was satiated only when he could become the disciple of his murshid (spiritual guide) Hazrat Nizamuddin Aulia.

Apart from the different Persian forms of poetry like *rubaee* and *masnavi*, Khusrau preferred the indigenous poetry in Hindi, Hindavi and Avadhi languages. His dohas often paint a lyrical miniature such as the one which he composed after the death of Hazrat Nizamuddin Aulia. Translated to

English: The fair beauty sleeps in the bed, hairs fallen to her face Khusrau, go home, evening has set in every direction.

Most remarkably, in his dohas and masnavis, Khusrau popularised the Sufi notion of unity of existence — Wahdatul Wajood — which draws parallel to the Vedanta philosophy of advaita. Like the Vedanta philosophy of advaita, the essence of Sufi doctrine of Wahdat-ul-Wujud is also universal. It exemplifies whatever exists in the universe as an aspect of divine reality diffused through different things. Thus, advaita and Wahdatul Wajud are two expressions of the only one essence.

Khusrau advanced the harmonious values of Indian culture with his focus on Khidmat-e-Khalq — service to mankind — a humane concept conceived by his master Hazrat Nizamuddin Aulia. He also promulgated the practice of sulh-e-kul. He stated: "Almighty holds dear those who love Him for the sake of human beings, and those who love human beings for the sake of Almighty."

Dewa's Divine Lover
Waris Piya & his Spiritual Consciousness

Sufi mystics like Waris Piya are vital to our collective spiritual consciousness……

Dewa Sharif, Hazrat Waris Ali Shah Dargah in Barabanki, UP India

Waris Ali Shah, more popularly known as Sarkar Waris Piya of Dewa Sharif, was an Indian Muslim mystic from Barabanki, a district in Uttar Pradesh. Besides an array of beautiful spiritual traits, Dewa Sharif is India's only dargah where Holi is celebrated as "Eid-e-Gulabi" with a similar fervour as in Hindu faith traditions.

Born into the 26th generation of Imam Hussain, Waris Piya was not an ordinary saint, but a successor to the prominent Sufi order — Qadriyya-Razzakiyya, and thus the founder of

Warsi Silsila in modern Indian Sufism. With a profound knowledge in classical Islamic sciences, Waris Piya was a widely travelled murshid (master) of people from across the country, irrespective of faith and creed. For decades, they all come together to celebrate the Sufi Holi as Eid-e-Gulabi at the sanctum of Dewa Sharif. A custodian of this dargah, Ghani Shah, asserts that Waris Piya exhorted his mureeds (disciples) to venerate every religion as a spiritual foundation based on the mutual feelings of love and devotion.

Ghafur Shah, a Warisi scholar, notes in his book: "The Blessed Lord Haji Hafiz Syed Waris Ali Shah," that Waris Piya undertook the Hajj pilgrimage several times, and held extensive visits to the West, especially the European countries, including Germany, England and Turkey. During his travels to Europe, Waris Piya also met and blessed the Sultan of Turkey and Bismarck of Berlin, and had an audience with Queen Victoria in England.

A close relative in Waris Pak's family lineage Prof. Wahajuddin Alwi, who is wedded to his great granddaughter, Asma Parween, tells us: "Since Waris Piya wanted people in India to transcend religious/sectarian divides, he participated in Hindu festivals like Holi. His non-Muslim mureeds and regular disciples included Raja Udit Narayan Sing, raja of Oudh, Thakur Pancham Singh talukdar of Eta, Pundit Deendaar Shah of Indore, Sahaj Ram Dixit, Thakur Grur Mohan Singh, a zamindar of Bhagalpur. They were spiritually in parallel with his Muslim bureaucrats such as governor general Ghulam Mohammad and Justice Sharfuddin."

Remarkably, Waris Piya allowed a mystical "gender fluidity" to flourish among his disciples. He did not deter women from entering his shrine. Though it caused him troubles from male chauvinists, he showed a sincere willingness for women's equal spiritual participation. Interestingly, it also happened to Baba Farid whose female disciple Bibi Fatima served as a senior teacher in his circle. But a male teacher became jealous of her and complained to Baba Farid: "How can you have a woman in our senior circle?" Baba Farid replied: "When the lion(ess) comes out of the jungle you had better run, you won't have time to tell whether it is a male or female lion!"

Shah-e-Hamadan
The saint who gifted Sufism to Kashmir

Dargah Hazratbal, Srinagar, Jammu & Kashmir, India

The people of Kashmir are indebted to Amir-i-Kabir Shah-e-Hamadan Mir Syed Ali Hamdani, may God bless him, precisely for two main reasons: firstly, for the promotion of actual Islam in the Valley and secondly for the development of a rich cultural tradition imbued in *Rishi-Sufism*. He was the proponent of Ibn al Arabi's idea of *Wahdatul Wajood*— Unity of the Being or Existence— and introduced it in the Valley of Kashmir with his insightful commentaries on his key texts *'Fusus al-Hikam'* and *'Al-Insan al-Kamal'*. Viewed from this philosophical perspective, many fountains of spiritual knowledge and mystical wisdom have sprung up in the current cultural setting of Kashmir from the writings and teachings of Shah e Hamdan.

The early period of the Shahmari dynasty is characterized by the fact that a large group of Sufi mystics from Central Asia, especially Sheikh Syed Ali Hamdani, entered the valley of Kashmir. He played a very pivotal role in the development of Islam in Kashmir and it is due to his efforts that Kashmir came to be known as 'Peer Wari'. Shah e Hamdan is also known as 'Amir e Kabir' as he is one of most prominent Sufi sages of the 14th century AD who belonged to the Kubrawiyya Silsilah, a significant Sufi lineage rooted in Central Asia. Through his teachings both in prose and poetry, Shah-e-Hamadan has shown the true love between the Creator (*Khaliq*) and the Created (*Makhlooq*). In his Sufi thoughts, he has laid greater emphasis on this divine and everlasting connection and thus has emphasized the spiritual salvation and ultimate liberation of an individual.

Shah e Hamdan's poetry touches various aspects of human life. It introduces us to the great principles of life and actually exposes us to the philosophy of life, which is why he deserves a unique place in the realm of Sufi Mystics and Muslim philosophers of the world. He not only played a key role in spreading Islam in Kashmir but also brought along with him various arts, handicrafts, modern sciences, cultural sciences, artefacts, pashminas and other crafts in the Kashmir Valley. He invited various experts, artisans and industrialists from Iran to present their art in Kashmir. Thus, a great social, cultural and economic revolution took place in Kashmir at the hands of Shah-e-Hamadan RA. Therefore, he is considered one of the great reformers of Islam who travelled to a large part of the known world in his service to mankind through the three main messages: Truth, Peace and Justice.

It is mentioned in historical records that Shah-e-Hamadan came along with 700 *Sadaat* or *Syedzadgaan* (the Prophet's progeny) who were exceptionally skilled companions. They introduced the local people of Kashmir to better and more profitable occupations such as carpet-weaving and shawl-weaving. These talented artisans taught the local population the codes of pashmina, textiles and carpet making. The state of Jammu and Kashmir, especially Ladakh, has greatly benefited from their active involvement and support in the textile industry. The development of the textile industry in Kashmir increased their importance, which led to a trend of migration from Kashmir to Ladakh, as a result of which a good number of Kashmiri Muslims settled in Ladakh, where they practiced writing, calligraphy and coinage as their prestigious professions. Art was thus introduced in Ladakh too at the hands of Sufi saints from Central Asia.

Shah-e-Hamadan accompanied by these Sadaat played an important role in the promotion of various handicraft activities and brought it from home to home in Kashmir. It is obvious that there was a dire need of talented people for the promotion of such professions and as a result, a large part of the society was provided with better jobs and employment. However, being a Sufi in principle, Shah-e-Hamadan did not attach much importance to worldly affairs and from a young age he abandoned materialism and took refuge in the bosom of Sufism.

In order to acquire mystical knowledge and attain perfection in Sufism, he acquired grace from his maternal uncle Hazrat Syed Alauddin Samnani RA, who was well-established as a great spiritual saint belonging to a noble Sufi lineage. Along with inner cleansing of his 'self' (Nafs) by undergoing an intense spiritual training and practical guidance from the Islamic luminaries of his times, Shah-e-Hamadan also had an inclination towards universal values and essential messages of Mysticism. He first augmented them travelling the world over around three times and then preached and promulgated them in the Valley of Kashmir.

Significantly, Shah-e-Hamdan work as a commentator on Ibn al Arabi's Wujudi philosophy played a key role in making him a well-known figure in South Asian Sufi literature. He had the special privilege of presenting the philosophy of Ibn Arabi in South Asia in local settings. Andalusia's Ibn al-Arabi or Ibn Arabi—commonly known as "Shaikh-e-Akbar" (the greatest Sufi master)—was one of the brightest Muslim mystics who rescued the soul of Islam from the clutches of literalist extremists. His religious thoughts and mystical theories propounded an inclusivist and pluralistic theology in the spirit of Sufism. He professed and practised Islam as the religion of unconditional love (*Muhabbat-e-Ghair Mashroot*) and as a spiritual path to eternal salvation through the prism of *Wahdat-ul-Wajud* (Unity of the Existence). Both his Deen (faith) and Shariat (law) were translated into an inclusive love and a wide embrace for one and all. Therefore, the extremist forces within Islam frowned upon his teachings, his intellectual moorings and the scholarly Sufi tradition he left behind, as they challenge the exclusivist and divisive sects and schools of thought even today.

As a matter of fact, Ibn Arabi's postulate of *Wahdatul Wujood* wielded great influence on Shah-e-Hamadan and later on other prominent Muslim mystics and Rishi-Sufi sages in the Valley. Most Rishi-Sufis in Kashmir—inspired by Shah-e-Hamadan—were actually *"Wujoodi"* (practitioners of the *Wahdat ul-Wujood* doctrine). They strongly believed that the light of the Creator is present in all Creations, and therefore, they taught their followers to respect people of all faith traditions. As a result, they were loved and admired by all and sundry. People of all castes and creeds, faiths and traditions were equally inspired by their concept of

Wahdat— Unity of Mankind and Oneness of God—which is an ultimate understanding of *Tawheed*.

Today, once again in the social, religious, cultural and economic milieu of Kashmir, the actual Sufi thoughts of Shah-e-Hamadan have to rule the roost. His balanced views of Islam are only a hopeful sign in the midst of a mutual friction of the Valley. He preached Islam in different parts of the world. But in Kashmir, he actually 'revived' and 'restored' Islam with the help of 700 Sadaat whose adherents sprang up as Rishi-Sufis. The way they undertook the gigantic task of *Dawat-e-Deen* in Kashmir, with their public gatherings, closed sermons, local writings and beautiful Sufi discourses, is greatly appreciated by world scholars, intellectuals and medieval historians. In his book "Haft Aqleem", Amir Ahmad Razi writes that Shah-e-Hamdan traveled around the world three times and met fourteen hundred saints. But in the end, it can be safely said, he chose the heaven on earth—Kashmir—as his last spiritual resort.

One cannot deny the fact that there is a greater need to revive the mystical thoughts of Shah-e-Hamdan today, not only to preserve the true Islamic teachings, but also to protect Islam from the clutches of evils. In the eyes of Shah-e-Hamdan, misinterpretation of Islam was the worst treatment meted out by the maulvis to the common Muslims under the false grabs which cannot be tolerated.

Lalded/Lalla Arifa
The Shaivite-Sufi Divine Lover

14th-century Rishi-Sufi revolutionary mystic Lal Ded, called 'Lalleshwari' by Hindus and 'Lalla Arifa' by Muslims unites the divided minds and hearts in the valley of Kashmir……..

I have seen an educated man starve,

A leaf blown off by bitter wind.

Once I saw a thoughtless fool beat his cook.

Lalla has been waiting for the allure of the world to fall away.

I might scatter the southern clouds,

Drain the sea, or cure someone hopelessly ill.

But to change the mind of a fool is beyond me.

One of the preceptors of mysticism in Kashmir was the celebrated female Sufi poet Lalla Arifa—popularly known as Lal Ded and Lal Diddi and Laleshwari. For around seven centuries, Lalla has been venerated both by Muslims and Hindus of Kashmir and is indisputably regarded as a proponent of a plural ethos in the valley.

Born in a brahmin family in 1335 AD near Srinagar, she renounced her domestic material life at the age of 24 after she suffered cruelty from her mother-in-law. Hence, she chose to be a devotee of the Shaivite saint Siddha Srikantha also known as Sed Bayu. She learnt from him high moral truths and thus practiced yoga philosophy. It is narrated that in her rebellious renouncement of domestic life, Lalla turned into a celibate mystic. However, when she met the Sufi mystic of the highest stature in Kashmir, Mir Syed Ali Hamadani, she gave up celibacy and began to wear purdah. Asked why, she said she had seen a man for the first time.

Sheikh-ul-Alam, another prominent Kashmiri Sufi mystic of the 14th century, gave the first direct reference to Lalla in his verse: That Lalla from Padmaanpora (Pampore), did drink nectar tumbler after tumbler. She was a saint and she did bring up a saint, O' God, give me her vision and knowledge. Remarkably, this Sufi-Shaivite lady rendered deep mystical experiences into her poetry which reveals her limitless devotion, spiritual illumination and her ecstasy of the divine union. She says in her Kashmiri poetry:

Yi yi karu'm suy artsun yi rasini vichoarum thi mantar yihay lagamo dhahas partsun suy Parasivun tanthar

Translation: Whatever work I did became worship of the Lord; Whatever word I uttered became a prayer; Whatever this body of mine experienced became the sadhana of Saiva Tantra illumining my path to Parmasiva).

At the same time, Lalla's poetry came crashing down on the parasitic forms of ritualism and false religiosity. She strongly believed in the Divine but equally discarded the priestly class. One of her verses reads: It covers your shame, keeps you from shivering. Grass and water are all the food it asks. Who taught you, priest-man, to feed this breathing thing to your thing of stone? In fact, the Shaivite mystics like Lalla and Sufi saints such as Shaikh-ul-A'alam strengthened unity in diversity in Kashmir's plural society for centuries.

While Shaikh-ul-A'alam was an ardent believer in Tawheed (monotheism), Lalla was a follower of the monotheistic Shaivism known as Turka Shastra. Albeit the difference in their spiritual disciplines, both believed in one Creator, loved all His creations, dismissed violent religious extremism, practised self-introspection and rejected all dogmatic and retrogressive ideologies. This was the result of an elevating experience of spiritual enlightenment. Prominent historian Azam Dedmari writes in his book, *Waqiat-e-Kashmir* (events in Kashmir): Lalla was buried in a tomb in the premises of the Sufi shrine of Baba Naseebuddin Gazi — a disciple of Sultan-ul-Arifeen Sheikh Hamza Makhdum.

Lalleshwari's beautiful and flowing Kashmiri poetry on divine love has been translated extensively into English, of late. This includes English translations by Jane Hirshfield in *Women in Praise of the Sacred: 43 Centuries of Spiritual Poetry by Women* (1994), Coleman Barks in *Naked Song: Lalla* (1992), and K.C.I.E. Sir George Grierson in *Lalla-Vakyani* or *The Wise Sayings of Lal-Ded, A Mystic Poetess of Ancient Kashmir* (1920).

Lal Ded's verses in Kashmiri called *vakh* shows her deep love for solitude. She left her heartbreaking marriage and took up a homeless life, as the legend goes. She went forth naked, dancing on the roads, singing her *vakh* as translated below:

My guru gave a single precept:

Turn your gaze from outside to inside

Fix it on the hidden self.

I, Lalla, took this to heart

And naked set forth to dance

Mahbub-ul-A'alam—Beloved of the World

Shrine of Makhdum Sahib on top of the Hari Parbat (Koh-e-Maran) Srinagar

Kashmir's Sufi mystic Hamza Makhdum—popularly known as *Makhdum Sahib*—and sometimes as *Sultan-ul-Arifeen* (king of the realised ones), is venerated in the Valley as the "Beloved of the World" (Mahbub-ul-Aalam). The 16th century pioneer of the Suhravard Sufi order in Kashmir belonged to a Chandravanshi Rajput family, and was born in a village near Sopore in Baramulla district. His spiritual hospice (Khanqah) and shrine is on top of the Hari Parbat (Koh-e-Maran), commanding a majestic view of the most beautiful part of Srinagar. According to several historians, Makhdum Sahib's family were descendants of Kangra's Rajput rulers, through Ramchandra — commander-in-chief in the army of Raja Suhadev, the last Hindu ruler of Kashmir, and minister in the court of Rinchen Shah, the first Muslim king of Kashmir.

Makhdum Sahib's entire lineage was known for an intellectual legacy and an ethics-based spirituality (Tariqat). In his childhood, his father Usman Raina, himself an acclaimed *A'alim* (scholar) taught him and then enrolled him in a Maktab at his village. Later, his grandfather, Reti Raina, took him to Srinagar, where he studied the classical Islamic sciences — from the Quran, Hadith, Kalam (philosophy), Fiqh (jurisprudence) to Sufism at Dar al-Shifa in Srinagar. Over there, Makhdum Sahib acquired the knowledge and gnosis of 14 different Sufi branches, but in his later life, he was more inclined towards the Suhrawardi Silsila (Sufi order) and adopted the spiritual path popularly known today as "Mahbubiyya Silsila" named after his epithet Mahbub-ul-Aalam (Beloved of the World). Thus, Makhdum Sahib became the first saint in the Valley who strengthened the common grounds for spiritual coexistence between the Rishis and Sufis in Kashmir.

Mahbub-ul-Aalam stressed the regular spiritual practice of *Zikr-e-Qalb* (inward remembrance of the Divine). He did not like the idea of outward flaunting of Zikr and, therefore, he exhorted Sufi music (Sim'a) only within the prescribed limits. Mahbub Sahib is also known for questioning the prevailing social customs and several superstitions like the blind faith in ghosts and the veneration of the spirits (muwakkils). Similarly, he did not reconcile with the idea of non-Suhrawardi orders about the seclusion and renunciation of worldly life. He contended that the renunciation does not imply going naked or forsaking worldly responsibilities. His idea of renunciation was one in which a seeker becomes more sincere on his/her path to the extent that even enormous wealth does not turn into an obstacle. He was one of the rarest Rishi-Sufis in the Valley who were sociable and accessible. Prior to him, the Sufi mystics in the Valley did not seem to have made significant social networks with the commoners. But Mahbub Sahib established a stronger base at the societal level and thus became the Mahbub-ul-Aalam (Beloved of the World) in the true sense. Mahbub Sahib met the Lord at the young age of 35 and he had lost all his teeth and all his hair had turned white. He would say:

"The pain of divine love (Gham-e-Ishq) has turned me old".

Kashmir's Nund Rishi— A Mystic Master for All

Ashakh suy yus ashkasatI daze
Son zan prazales pananuy pan
Ashkun nar yes valinji saze
Ada mali vatiy suy lamakan.

Translation:

The body exposed to the cold river winds blowing,

Thin porridge and half-boiled vegetable to eat-

There was a day, O Nasaro!

My spouse by my side and a warm blanket to cover us,

A sumptuous meal fish to eat-

There was a day, O Nasaro!

14th-century mystic Sheikh Noor-ud-din Wali — widely known as Nund Rishi— was the founder of Rishi-Sufi order in Kashmir and an epitome of Divine Love in the valley. While Muslims revere him as *Sheikh-ul-Aalam* (mentor for all), Hindus often call him *Sahaj Anand* (affectionate soul)…..

As evidenced above, rich in spiritual and mystical intellect, Kashmir's Rishi-Sufis spoke in poetry, allegories and parables to highlight the universal human trajectories. The valley of Kashmir has been one of the sacrosanct places for mystics. Historically, it was the bastion of pluralism, which merged the two Indian Oceans of mysticism — Rishimat and Sufism — thus introducing "Rishi-Sufis" as harbingers of mutual respect, understanding, spiritual acceptance and non-violence.

Kashmiriyat—a philosophy of pluralism and peaceful coexistence—has been propounded by the Rishi-Sufi mystics. Kashmir has been the land of Mystics—from Rishimunis to the Rishi Sufis. A 5,000-year-old civilisation, Kashmir is an inherent part and parcel of the idea of India. It is Kashmir where various faith traditions of India including Hinduism, Buddhism, and Sufi Islam converged in a spiritual synergy. In the 1st millennium BC, Kashmir was the centre of Buddhism and Shaivism. It was in Kashmir where the 4th Buddhist Council was held and great scholars like Vasumitra, Ashvaghosha, and Nagarjuna participated. It was in Kashmir where India's first original work on history titled "Rajatarangani" by Kalhan was written. And it was in Kashmir where the Persianate and pluralistic version of Islam emerged with the coming of Sufi saints from Central Asia. The Muslim phase of Kashmir began in 1300 AD with the Buddhist ruler Rinchana's conversion to Islam.

The syncretic traditions of religious pluralism have been so deep in the valley that even when the entire country was afflicted with the partition on religious lines, the Kashmiris were basking in the glory of its communal harmony and religious diversity. Even in the 1970s when Islamist nationalism was on the march in Pakistan and in the 1980s when Hindu nationalism was taking root in India, it was Kashmir where the syncretic culture still flourished.

Until the late 1980s, both Kashmiri Pandits and Muslims have jointly participated in festivals like Kheer Bhawani, Amarnath Yatra, and shrine visitation of Charar-e-Sharif. Although a few extremists in the valley tried to sabotage the valley's distinct syncretic culture, the common Kashmiris have been imbued with the pluralist Rishi-Sufi tradition. Muslims in Jammu and Kashmir have been known for their wide embrace of the Hindu and Buddhist cultural practices. This is why their version of Sufism is distinctly known as Rishi-Sufism. Lal Ded—the celebrated Sufi-Shaivite saint— has been venerated both by Hindus and Muslims of Kashmir and is still seen in the valley as a major proponent of a plural society. While Muslims call her "Lalla Arifa", Hindus recall her as Laleshwari. For around seven centuries, Lalded has been popularly known for the Kashmiri legacy of religious pluralism. Similarly, the 14th-century Kashmiri mystic — Sheikh Noor-ud-din Wali — who is widely known as Nund Rishi, is revered by Muslims as Sheikh-ul-Aalam (mentor of all), while Hindus revere him Sahaj Anand (affectionate soul).

The founder of Rishi-Sufi order in Kashmir and the 14th-century Muslim mystic — Sheikh Noor-ud-din Wali —

widely known as Nund Rishi was an epitome of Divine Love in the valley. While Muslims revere him as *Sheikh-ul-Aalam* (mentor for all), Hindus often call him *Sahaj Anand* (affectionate soul).

Born in 1377, he was bestowed with mystical moorings right from his childhood days. His foster mother was a female mystic (yogini) popularly known as Lal Ishwari among Hindus and Lal Arifa among Muslims. Holding the newborn Nund Rishi in her lap, she whispered in Kashmiri in his ear to feed him with her milk:

Chai ali chai zaina yali na mandchookh chaina kyazi chukh mandchaan

(Suckle son, suckle, you didn't hesitate when you were born, why hesitate now?)

Inspired by the early Kashmiri mystics, Nund Rishi strengthened the Valley's syncretic culture spreading his messages in the form of verses and poetry. Most verses by Sheikh-ul-Alam or Nund Rishi foster the concept of *ishq-e-haqiqi* (divine love) and *wisal-e-ilahi* (divine union), such as these:

Oh God, you are all pervading,

You are the self in our body.

When man's heart lights up with the flame of love,

Then shall he reach La-Makaan (no-place).

First I forgot myself and yearned after God,

Then I reached La-Makaan (the highest mystical state).

Many such verses in Nund Rishi's poetry build a deeper personal relationship with God and inevitably an innate concern for all his creations — mankind, animals, nature and environment in particular. Therefore, his poetry is popularly known as "Shrukhs" (catholicity of vision). Significantly, environmental protection and preservation of the Valley's nature from devastation is also the thrust of his verses like this:

Extensively I toured in jungles through kail trees,

The warmth of June touched adversely the delicacy of jasmine,

Distinct are not the pearls to the moisture,

Mere touch shall damage delicacy of diamond,

Sooner the flame of tulips shall extinguish,

The evening occasions but the drowsiness of slumber.

Thus, Nund Rishi or Sheikh-ul-Aalam left deep spiritual imprint in the teachings of later Rishi-Sufis of the Kashmir valley like Hamza Makhdoom also known as Mehboob-ul-Alam (loved by all), Shamas Faqir, the celebrated Kashmiri Sufi poet and Resh Mir Sahib, a prolific Sufi scholar called the "last giant of the Rishi-Sufism".

Rishi-Sufis focused not only on spiritual pursuits but also social, economic and cultural development of the Kashmir Valley. In fact, they brought the various crafts and industries from Persia, like the famous pashmina, the textiles woven in Kashmir. Today's Valley is in search of the very lost cultural heritage. In the words and verses (Kashmiri *vakhas*) of Nund Rishi:

Poshini poshivariy garan

Mogul garan huniy vas

Shaj shinalay garan

Khar garan guh led ta sas

The oriole seeks out a flower garden;

The owl seeks out a deserted spot;
The she-jackal searches dreary wastes;
The donkey searches dung and dirt.

Ghaus Gwaliyari—The Shattari-Sufi Mystic

Tomb of Muhammad Ghaus Gawaliyari in Gwalior, MP India

Little is known about the story of the 16th century Indian Sufi mystic Shah Muhammad Ghaus of Gawalior. He was a proponent of Silsila Shattariyya in India, founded by the 15th century Persian Sufi saint Sirajuddin Abdullah Shattar.

Besides a Shattari-Sufi pioneer, Ghaus Gwaliyari was one of the first translators of yoga texts to Persian in the 16th century. Gwalior's Sufi mystic, musician and an epoch-making philosopher Muhammad Ghaus Gwaliyari left behind an indelible legacy of syncretic Indian culture in his literature. His spiritual insights guided the lives and thoughts of Indian Muslims over a thousand years and are glaring evidence of how Sufi mystics engaged with India's cultural practices, not only with their participation in art, culture and literature, but also through the experience of various forms of yoga. A lot of Indian Sufi practices based on self-awareness can be considered yogic in nature, although yoga is defined differently from myriad perspectives.

The 16th century Sufi saint Ghaus Gwaliyari was the earliest Indian proponent of Silsila Shattariyya — the 15th century Persian Sufi order founded by Sirajuddin Abdullah Shattar. Etymologically, shattar, an Arabic-origin Persian word meaning "lightning" denotes a code of spiritual practices that lead to a state of "completion". No wonder then, the Sufi order of Shattariyya originated in Persia but was codified and completed in India, the land of thousands of mystics.

Besides being a Shattari Sufi pioneer, Ghaus Gwaliyari was one of the first translators of Yoga texts to Persian in the 16th century. Before Gwaliyari, Shaikh Abdul Quddus Gangohi (1456–1537), who ranks as an eminent Sufi poet from the Sabiri order, was familiar with yoga texts and traditions in India like the yoga of the Naths — a Shaivism-related yogic practice which emerged around the 13th century. Like Hatha Yoga, the practice of Nath is particularly used to transform one's body into a state of awakened self-identity with absolute reality (Sahaja Siddha). Through the lineage of the Nath yogis, the science of Kundalini Kriya Yoga has been preserved in India through the corridors of time.

Sufi mystics like Sheikh Abdul Quddus Gangohi and Shah Muhammad Ghaus Gwaliyari endeavoured to uphold the age-old Indian legacy. They practiced and preached the yoga, though it drew controversy from a few fundamentalist clergymen who considered yoga to be incompatible with their puritanical religious moorings. On account of such syncretic ideas and practices, Gwaliyari was vehemently opposed by the orthodox ulema. But he did not give up and carried on with his hard work of translations of yoga texts into Persian, which were later rendered into Arabic, Turkish and Urdu.

One of the most notable translations of yogic texts rendered by Gwaliyari is Bahr al-Hayat or The Ocean of Life — a Persian translation and explanation of Amrtakunda — one of the key Sanskrit texts on yoga.

This remarkable Persian translation was rendered in the city of Broach in Gujarat in 1550 and was basically aimed at explaining the Hawd al-Hayat (The Pool of Life), which is the first Arabic translation of Amrtakunda. It occupied a paramount significance in the oral traditions and teachings of the Shattari Sufis in India to the extent that it became a textbook for many of Gwaliyari's followers. Another work by Gwaliyari which highlights close resemblances between the Shattari Sufi practices and yogic exercises is *Jawahir-e-Khamsa* (The Five Jewels), which was later translated to Arabic by a Mecca-based Shattari teacher, Sibghat Allah. In this treatise, Gwaliyari dwelled upon his mystical experience of ascension which enabled him to hold conversations even with the Divine. His two famous books *Jawahir-e-Khamsa* which contains five chapters including one on the worship of God and *Bahr-e-Hayat* (the ocean of life) which sheds light on the yogic secrets of life, are jeweled lights in Sufi mysticism. *Bahr-e-Hayat* is actually his translation and extension of *Hawd al-Hayat* (The Pool of Life), an Arabic translation of a lost Sanskrit text on yoga, the *Amrtakunda*. Shah Gawaliyari died in 15 Ramadan 970 AH, and his Dargah, holy shrine is called Gwalior Sharif located in Madhya Pradesh.

Dard's Divine Poetics

"Ma'rifat is the secret (*sirr*) connected to the essence (*kunh*) of each reality (*haqiqat*), and Haqiqat is the secret of the secrets (*sirr-e-sirr*)"...

~Khwaja Mir Dard (1720-1785)

Sair Kar Duniya Ki Ghafil Zindagani Phir Kahan,
Zindagi Gar Kuch Rahi To Yeh Jawani Phir Kahan!
— Khwaja Mir Dard

Khwaja Mir Dard was among Delhi's most prominent Sufi mystics and Urdu poets. Born in 1721, he was spiritually inclined since his childhood and was trained by his father Khwaja Nasir Andaleeb, himself a mystic of the Naqshbandi Sufi order and a noted poet. Having completed an informal elementary education at home, Dard attained the spiritual companionship of the Sufi luminaries well-versed in Arabic and Persian studies. But he did not get content with his existing knowledge of theology, philosophy and languages. He developed a very good flair for Sufi music with the renowned Sufi singers (Qawaals) who frequented his father's house. Dard believed that mastering the art of expression is a God-gifted skill and a mark of "manhood" (adamiyat). Thus, he draws a close resemblance between learning the art of speech and possessing humanity. Dard strongly believed that his own poetry was divinely inspired through *kashf* (unveiling) — a Gnostic Sufi doctrine dealing with knowledge of the heart rather than of the intellect.

It is held in Sufism that *kashf* and *ilham* (divine unveiling or inspiration) are bestowed on the saints as an immense spiritual force through which they express their divine love, wisdom or knowledge in prose or poetry. But they are obtainable only through the purification of the heart by constant remembrance (*zikr*) of the divine. However, ilham is completely distinct from wah'y (divine revelation), which is exclusive to the prophets. Notably, Dard's claim of the divine origin for his poetry did not go down well with many of the contemporary clerics who rejected it outright as a poetic illusion.

However, Dard did not proclaim it without walking in the Sufi path of the four stages: (1) Shariat (revealed law), (2) Tariqat (spiritual path), (3) Marifat (gnosis) and (4) Haqiqat (reality). He encapsulates this spiritual process: "Shariat is the form of Haqiqat and the latter is the inner meaning of the former. While Tariqat implies being characterised by the Shariat, Marifat is the unveiling of the Haqiqat. Thus, Shariat is the external form of Sufism and Tariqat is the inner level. However, Marifat is the secret (*sirr*) connected to the essence (*kunh*) of each reality, and Haqiqat is the secret of the secrets (*sirr-e-sirr*).

At the young age of 28, Dard literally renounced the worldly pleasures and became one of the major mystic poets of Delhi, including Mir Taqi Mir and Mirza Sauda. Thus, he is recalled today as one of the three pillars of the classical Urdu ghazal (a type of amatory Urdu poems originating in Arabic and Persian). Dard wrote many ghazals with deeply mystical meanings. These couplets largely convey the message that the world is a phenomenal veil of eternal reality. One of his beautiful couplets that can be read to understand his divine connection and mystical inclination, is as follows

Dosto dekha tamasha yahan ka bus

Tum raho khush hum to apne ghar chale

Translation: My friend, we have seen enough of this play. We are going home, you can stay.

Aaina-e-Hind—The Divine Radiance in Bengal

The 14th century Sufi mystic of Bengal, Syed Akhi Usman Sirajuddin, popularly known as Akhi Siraj is greatly revered as "Aaina-e-Hind" (mirror of Hindustan). One of the spiritual vicegerents of Hazrat Nizamuddin Aulia, Akhi also attained closeness with Baba Fariduddin and acquired through spiritual knowledge from Shaikh Fakhruddin Zarradi. He founded the Chishti mystic tradition in Bengal where his dargah in Gaur, West Bengal attracts great visitations. In fact, the first Sufi hospice (khanqah) in Bengal was established by Akhi Siraj. In Bengal, he had prominent disciples and successors like Hazrat Ala-ul-Haq of Pandua and Hazrat Amir Khurd. It is mentioned in Siyar-ul-Auliya, a Persian biography of India's Chishti Sufi saints that Akhi Siraj "illuminated the whole region with his spiritual radiance". The local Bengali people had so much love and veneration for him that they called him "Piran-e-Pir" (the saint of saints), an epithet generally attributed to Baghdad's greatest Sufi saint, Abdul Qadir Jilani.

An extremely modest Sufi, Akhi Siraj spent all his short-lived life in the wider dissemination of spiritual intellect in the vast land of Bengal. His teachings left an everlasting impact on the syncretic culture and belief of Muslims in Bengal. As a result, most Bengali Muslims adhere to the spiritual strain of Islam even today. As the true "mirror of India", his spiritual light radiated from his discourses on divine knowledge and illuminated the whole region.

Prominent saints of Bengal quenched their thirst from the spiritual fountain of *Aaina-e-Hind*. Some of his disciples belonged to the aristocratic families with close relations to the government of Sultan Shamsuddin Ilyas Shah. But he taught them to live the modest life of a Sufi. He sought to change the elitist ways of his upper-class murids (disciples). For instance, Ala-ul-Haq whose father was the treasurer of the provincial government in Bengal was enjoined to humble himself by walking with a hot cauldron on his head. In his devotion to his master, Ala-ul-Haq would carry a cauldron of hot food on his head even though it would burn his hair.

It is mentioned in *Akhbar-ul-Akhyar*, a famous Persian treatise on Sufism: Once a dervish from Suharwardi Sufi order came to spend time with Akhi Siraj. He noticed that after the night prayer (isha), Akhi Siraj went to bed, while he himself was busy praying and supplicating all night. But in the morning, he was doing namaz (fajr) without ablution (wuzu). Seeing this, the dervish said, "I am surprised that you were asleep all night and now you pray without ablution!" Siraj replied in a remarkable Persian couplet:

Agar ashiq beh masjid dar nayamad

Dil-e-ashiq hamesha dar namaz ast

Translation: The heart of a true lover — Ashiq — is always in worship, even if he doesn't attend a mosque for a prayer.

Bu Ali Shah Qalandar—
Fragrance of Ali Maula

Ghulam-i-Roo-e Ou Boodam, Aseer-i-Boo-e Ou Boodam

Ghubar-i-Koo-e Ou Boodam, Nami Danam Kuja Raftam

(Diwan E Hazrat Sharafuddeen Bu Ali Qalandar)

Translation: I fell in love with him as a slave of his face, and I find myself captivated by his beautiful fragrance and scent. I became a dust on his street, and I do not know where I am moving.

Shaikh Sharafuddin Bu Ali Shah Qalandar RA is indeed the scent and fragrance of Prophet Muhammad (pbuh) and his Wali (substitute) Imam Ali A.S in India. No wonder why the holy Prophet (pbuh) reportedly said: I find a fragrance and the scent of heaven coming from the dust of Hind (India). He also felt a cool breeze coming from Hindustan, as reported in a hadith and encapsulated in an Urdu couplet by Allama Iqbal:

Meer-e-Arab (ﷺ) Ko Aayi Thandi Hawa Jahan Se

Mera Watan Wohi Hai, Mera Watan Wohi Hai

Saints are the scents of Imam Ali A.S—the head of Islamic sainthood [Wilayat]—especially in the Indian subcontinent. Among those Indian Sufi Mystics, Shaikh Sharafuddin Bu Ali Shah Qalandar famously known as "Bu Ali" (the fragrance of Imam Ali A.S) was born in Panipat in 1209 AD (605 AH), the present-day Haryana, India, where his tomb is also situated and venerated today both Muslims and non-Muslims of the country.

He was one of the descendants of Imam e Aazam Abu Hanifa Numan Bin Sabit—a spiritual heir, student and disciple of Imam Ja'afar e Sadiq AS, who was a descendant of the holy Prophet (pbuh). It is also said that he was the cousin of Sheikh Jamaluddin Ahmad Hanswi, a direct descendant of Imam Abu Hanifa, and a renowned Persian jurist of Islam who was born at Ghazni, (Khorasan). Bu Ali Shah Qalandar's father was Syed Muhammad Abul Hassan Fakharuddin also known as *"Fakhar e Alam"* and was a great scholar and saint of his time, and his mother Bibi Fatima was also a prominent mystic.

The reason why he was called "Bu Ali Qalandar" was touching to know. Since childhood, the young Sharfuddin had a deep wish. He prayed for Imam Ali A.S to reincarnate in him i.e. he wanted and strived to embody the life and teachings and persona of Syedna Imam Ali A.S. One day, he met a Saint who told him the truth: 'Ali is only One. No one can take his place'. So, you can't get to his position. However, you will be blessed with his fragrance and spiritual scent. Since then, the Qalandar became intoxicated by the fragrance of Imam Ali A.S, and from that day he started calling himself "Bu Ali". Later on, he came to learn that the Saint he met was none other than Ali A.S himself. This ignited his inner mystical world which was filled with the passion and adoration of Imam Ali A.S, as he enumerates in a Persian couplet:

Haidariyyam Qalandaram Mastam, Banda e Murtaza Ali Hastam,

Peshwa-e-Tamam Rindaanam, Keh Sag e Koo-e-Sher-i-Yazdanam

Translation: I am Haydari Qalandar [a mystic of Maula Ali]. I live in servitude to Ali Murtaza. I am the Master of all those who are intoxicated with him, and I'm like a dog roaming around the lanes of Allah's Lion.

According to the famous historical Urdu document on the Saints of Indian Subcontinent *Tazkira-e-Awliya-e-Hind-o-Paak*, once Hazrat Ali (*Karramallahu Wajhahu*) rescued him out of a river. Since then, he became intoxicated with the spiritual state of Jazb and ecstasy. He began to live in an ecstatic state of absorption (*Mast-o-Alast*) all the time, and hence he is called "*Qalandar e Haydari*" (the Mystic of *Haider e Karrar*).

Once, Hazrat Bu Ali Shah Qalandar was teaching his students in the historical mosque "**Masjid Quwwat Ul Islam**" as usual. Suddenly a dervish passed by. He stood in front of Bu Ali Shah Qalandar and chanted the Divine Name three times in a loud and clear voice. Bu Ali became silent and started looking at him. Then the dervish addressed him directly and said: Sharafuddin, recall the purpose for which Allah has sent you to this world. Why did you forget that? You should first finish the work you came to complete. Then you can keep teaching. The magic in the words of this dervish captivated Bu Ali Shah Qalandar at that very moment, and he said goodbye to all his students. They kept running after him but he rushed and disappeared. Out of his state of absorption (*Jazb-o-Masti*), he started traveling and wandering from town to town. If he spent his morning somewhere, his evening would be somewhere else. Most of the time, he was fasting. At the time of breaking the fast, he would eat only a little or leftover. Otherwise he would break his fast with just a glass of water. In this condition, Bu Ali Shah Qalandar went outside India and thus he came across the two great Saints—Mevlana Jalaluddin Rumi and his Murshid Hazrat Shams Tabrizi, who honoured him with a *Jubba* (robe) and tied a turban (*Dastar*) on his head.

Hazrat Bu Ali Qalandar was keenly fond of poetry. Often he used to compose and recite poems in Persian. On some occasions, he also recited Fil Badeeh Ash'ar (extempore poems) and surprised the audience. His Persian poetry is still quenching the thirst of spiritual seekers who are greatly benefiting from his writings—collected in Masnavi Bu Ali Qalandar— especially on Divine Love (Ishq-e-Ilahi). Take a glimpse:

"Open your eyes and hearts and look carefully at what the Lover (the Divine) has created for you with His *Ishq* (love) and how He has shown it so clearly. He decorated a tree with His beauty and produced different kinds of fruits. He put a taste in each fruit. A tree is neither aware of its own nature nor its flowers nor its fruits. He has created for you sweet sugar which might not be aware of its sweetness. He put musk in the navel of the deer for your sake, and the deer itself does not know about it. He created amber for you from the sea cow, and fragrance for you with musk. He produced camphor for you from the tree, while the tree itself does not know camphor. But if you know yourself well, everything will be recognized within you".

A collection of his letters to his disciples has appeared in the book form. These letters are a prime text on the topic of

"*Tawheed*" (Oneness of God). In short, the code is rich in unity and knowledge. His book, Diwan-e- Sharafuddin Bu Ali Qalandar is a great collection of poetry on Divine Love in Persian. His Persian poems include *Ghazals*, quatrains, and other genres.

Tellingly, Bu Ali Shah Qalandar was also a lover of Delhi's Divine Lover—Aashiq Allah Hazrat Sheikh Shahabuddin, a Mureed and Khalifa of Khwaja Qutbuddin Bakhtiar Kaki RA. It is also said that he himself was a disciple and caliph of Qutbuddin Bakhtiar Kaki. Some maintain that he was the Khalifa of Sheikh Najamuddin Qalandar. Hazrat Bu Ali Qalandar passed away on the 13th of Ramadan 724 AH (September 1324). His close disciple and caliph, Hazrat Makhdoom Latifuddin Danishmand, became a Sufi sage of great merit, whose shrine is situated in Morah Talab, Bihar Sharif.

Bulleh Shah—
Pierced by An Arrow of Divine Love

Baba Bulleh Shah (Representational Image)

Alif Allah ratta dil mera!

Alif Allah naal ratta dil mera

Meno "Bay" di khabar na kai

Translation: The invocation and contemplation of the name and essence of Allah—Zaat-e-ilahi—has immersed me so deeply in Divine Love that I no longer know anything about anything else except Him.

Baba Bulleh Shah—originally named by his parents as 'Abdullah Shah'— is aptly known as the "King of the Divine

Lovers" (*Sultan-ul-Ashiqeen*) in the vast Sufi literature in Urdu and Persian in the Indian subcontinent.

This Punjabi Sufi mystic of the Indian subcontinent lived from 1680 to 1757 in what is now Pakistan. Significantly, his beautiful poetic exhortations of unconditional love and harmony are more relevant today in every conflict-ridden country and communally vitiated atmosphere. He believed that only in wahdat-ul-wujud (unity of all beings in the divine) and that too at an experiential and not just theoretical level, one can go beyond the man-made boundaries. His Punjabi poetry shows us a clear trajectory towards this ultimate reality.

In this regard, there is an excellent book, *Bulleh Shah: Sufi Lyrics*, translated by Christopher Shackle that I recently had the good fortune to go through. This is a striking modern English version of the beautiful Punjabi lyrics presented alongside the Punjabi text in the Gurmukhi script. Because of his lucid poetic style through popular musical genres, Bulleh Shah is still endeared to Muslims, Hindus and Sikhs both in India and Pakistan as well as in the international Punjabi diaspora.

Sadly, Bulleh Shah suffered the fanatic persecution even after his demise. The local clergy did not allow the burial of his dead body in the graveyard. Three days passed after his death, but he was not buried. His body was taken outside for burial. But his divine union found resonance across the world:

I have been pierced by the arrow of love, what shall I do?

I can neither live, nor can I die. I have peace neither by night, nor by day.

The fire of separation is unceasing! Let someone take care of my love.

In an easy local Punjabi language, Bulleh Shah's poetry has amazed the wider world of mysticism with a deep and lasting impact. Take a look:

Sir-e chanaan ae pand azabaan di

Kyun hui ae shakl jalaadaan di

Ayeh peinda mushkil bhaara ae

Ik Alif parho chhutkara ae

Translation: Why do you read so many books? Why do you bear the burden of sorrows on your head? Why have you taken on such a harsh, tyrannical appearance? The journey to the next world is very difficult. By studying the lesson of *Ism-Allah* (Divine Name) and *Zaat* (Divine Essence), you will find deliverance from every agony, sorrow and grief.

Blessings for the Book

On their journey of seeking the truth, each seeker not only inevitably explores the essence of Sufism but also takes some guidance from it at some point. Like the Urdu language, Sufism, too, has had its roots in India for more than a century now.

When our dependency on social media for (mis)information is increasing by leaps and bounds, we are becoming so irrational, even standing on the top rung of the evolutionary ladder, that we are on the verge of stopping using our minds. Very few of us know that countless words we use in our daily dialect are Urdu and have originated from Arabic, Persian or Turkish. For example, some Arabic words are *aadami* (man), *aurat* (woman), *umra* (age), and *kitab* (book); some of the commonly used Persian words are *chashma* (glasses), *chehara* (face), *zeher* (poison), and *shadi* (marriage); and a few of the Turkish words heavily used in India are *bahadur* (brave), *kurta* (long shirt), *chaqu* (knife), *chammach* (spoon), etc. Urdu language also showcases the Ganga-Jamuni Tehzeeb, also known as Hindustani Tehzeeb, which is a composite culture that combines Hindu and Muslim cultural elements in the central plains of northern India, especially the Doab region of the Ganges and Yamuna rivers. As we proceed in the twenty-first century, we must not forget that the Ganga-Jamuni Tehzeeb has given us many freedom fighters to expel the Britishers from our beloved nation and taste freedom.

Noted Indian Muslim scholar and Sufi poet Maulana Syed Fazl-ul-Hasan Hasrat Mohani coined the slogan 'Inquilab

Zindabad'. The Sufi poets, deeply rooted in their spiritual journey, have long held Lord Rama and Lord Krishna in the highest regard, their verses resonating with the divine essence of these revered figures.

In a time when most people are stuck in the boundaries of concepts and labels, this work by the mystic author, poet, translator, and Indo-Islamic Scholar Mr Ghulam Rasool Dehlvi is like a refreshment for thinkers. This book, a collection of articles he wrote over a few years, throws light on the century of Sufi saints, mystics, scholars and poets that flourished in the land of Bharat.

Best wishes to Ghulam ji for the success of *Ishq Sufiyana*.

- **Dr Medhavi Jain**

Founder, Dharma For Life

Author, Poet and Life Coach

This book brings alive inspired Sufis—their stories and poetry—in the rich traditions of mystical love. Ghulam's translation-mastery dances in language! It's a treasure chest of Sufi reflection.... opened and revealed here.

- **Tamam Kahn**

Pirani of the Sufi Ruhaniat International

Author of "Untold, A History of the Wives of Prophet Muhammad"

In "Ishq Sufiyana: Untold Stories of Divine Love", Ghulam Rasool Dehlvi, takes us on a journey into the mystical world of Sufism to explore the Concept of Divine Love, where love for the Divine transcends all earthly bounds. Through an exploration of poetry, teachings, and the lives of renowned Sufi mystics, discover how the passionate pursuit of divine union shapes the soul and illuminates the path to spiritual fulfillment.

- **Rana Safvi**
Renowned Writer, Scholar & Translator
Author of In Search of the Divine

In a time when love is often seen through the lens of convenience and fleeting passion, 'Ishq Sufiyana' presents an enchanting odyssey into the realms of mystic love that transcends the earthly and touches the divine.

From the outset, Ghulam Rasool Dehlvi immerses readers through poetic prose and evocative storytelling, teachings, and reflections of Sufi scholars from the Indian subcontinent - each being a thread that guides the reader through the journey from Ishq-e-Majazi to Ishq-e-Haqiqi.

A timeless piece that resonates with readers long after the last page is turned!

- **Dr Ruchika Arora**
Researcher, Writer and Editor
PhD in Architecture from England

"Ishq Sufiyana" is not just a book; it is a spiritual companion for those seeking to deepen their connection with the Divine and embrace the spirit of love, service, and unity in their lives. Whether you are a seasoned practitioner or a curious soul, this book offers a gateway to the mystical world of Sufism and the enduring legacy of various Sufi Orders.

May this journey of unconditional love and devotion inspire and illuminate your path.

- **Hazrat Syed Mohammad Ashraf Kichhouchhwi**

Founder & Chairman, World Sufi Forum

"Ishq Sufiyana" is a profound exploration of the divine love and spiritual ecstasy that lies at the heart of Sufism. Through the lens of the Chishty Sufi Order, this book delves into the transformative power of Ishq (love) and how it shapes the soul's journey towards the Divine.

Drawing from the rich heritage of Hazrat Khwaja Moinuddin Chishty (RA) and the sublime teachings of Khidmat-e-Khalq (service to mankind), Ghulam Rasul Dehlvi put forth an insight on the path of a Sufi seeker. With heartfelt reflections and historical insights, "Ishq Sufiyana" brings to life the essence of Peace towards all and the universal message of love and compassion that transcends religious boundaries.

- **Haji Syed Salman Chishty**

Gaddi Nashin, Dargah Ajmer Sharif

Chairman, Chishty Foundation

www.ingramcontent.com/pod-product-compliance
Lightning Source LLC
LaVergne TN
LVHW041606070526
838199LV00052B/3014